Pedrito's World

# Pedrito's World

Arturo O. Martínez

Texas Tech University Press

This book is typeset in Adobe Garamond. The paper used in this book meets the minimum requirements of ANSI/NISO Z39.48-1992 (R1997). ∞

*Library of Congress Cataloging-in-Publication Data*
Martínez, Arturo O., 1933-
    Pedrito's world / Arturo O. Martínez.
      p. cm.
    Summary: In southern Texas in 1941, six-year-old Pedrito holds onto his hope for a better future as he helps to grow watermelons on his parents' farm and sell them in San Antonio, and attends school five miles from home.
    ISBN-13: 978-0-89672-600-0 (lithocase : alk. paper)
    ISBN-10: 0-89672-600-2 (lithocase : alk. paper)
    [1. Farm life—Texas—Fiction. 2. Family life—Texas—Fiction. 3. Schools—Fiction. 4. Mexican Americans—Fiction. 5. Texas—History —1865–1950—Fiction.] I. Title.
PZ7.M367127Ped 2007
[Fic]—dc22

                                        2006021628


Printed in the United States of America
07 08 09 10 11 12 13 14 15 / 9 8 7 6 5 4 3 2 1
MG

Texas Tech University Press
Box 41037
Lubbock, Texas 79409-1037 USA
800.832.4042
ttup@ttu.edu
www.ttup.ttu.edu

*The tales in this book are all real, as far as I can remember. The characters have been invented, based on real people. Many loved ones from my childhood days are no longer with us and no longer able to tell us the stories of their suffering, their joys, and their hardships: among them my parents, Gabriel and Martina, my brothers Gabriel and Joel, and my sister Olga. To them I dedicate this book, as well as to my wife, Pat, my children, Nora and Peter, and my other brothers and sisters, Angelita, Urbana, Rubén, and Lisandro.*

# Contents

# Preface

In 1941 the Japanese attacked Pearl Harbor. The United States declared war on Germany, Italy, and Japan. President Roosevelt began his third term in office. Joe Louis was the World Heavyweight boxing champion. The Yankees defeated the Brooklyn Dodgers in the World Series. The horse Whirlaway won the Kentucky Derby and went on to capture the Triple Crown. *How Green Was My Valley* won the Academy Award for best picture of the year and *Citizen Kane* was one of the most controversial. *The Keys of the Kingdom* was probably the most popular book in years.

But these people and places and events were far removed from my little world. I was a six-year-old kid living on a small farm in South Texas. Except for a trip to San Antonio, a five-hour drive to the north, my life was the farm and the school I attended in a village a few miles away. Mine was a far different, simpler little world. Let me tell you something about it, as far as I can remember.

# Acknowledgments

My father died when I was only seven years old, and there were some very difficult years while I was growing up. But in spite of it all, my mother, Martina, along with my seven sisters and brothers, insisted that I receive the best education possible.

Several teachers at Rio Grande City High School, particularly Olive Hinojosa and Emma Solis, detected a love for writing and reading within me and encouraged me to develop in that direction. My writing teachers at Marquette University's College of Journalism took this raw kid from South Texas and prepared him for a joyous career in a very exciting field. Two of the best newspaper editors I encountered during my many years in journalism were most encouraging. Vince Marino at the *Lafayette (La.) Advertiser* made sure I had the proper word or phrase to tell a story, even if it killed us both. The late Mort Pye at the *Star-Ledger* in Newark, New Jersey, where I worked for thirty years, gave me many challenges as an editor and writer, trusting me to slave over and edit very difficult news stories, essays, and critical works by some excellent (and some not so excellent) writers.

Catherine Hapka, a children's book editor, read an early version of *Pedrito's World* and made some very valuable suggestions. Judith Keeling, my editor at Texas Tech University Press, has been a one-person cheering section, offering much advice and encouragement.

My children, Peter and Nora, who wanted to learn about my heritage, jogged my memory of my childhood stories, thus planting the seeds for this book. Finally, my wife, Pat, an excellent editor, saw a book lurking among those stories and was more responsible than anyone else for encouraging, cajoling, suggesting, and sweet-talking me into action.

To all of them I am deeply indebted. But not one of the above can be faulted with any failings the reader may detect in *Pedrito's World*.

ARTURO O. MARTÍNEZ

# Pedrito's World

# Chapter 1

## San Antonio, Here We Come

"Pedrito, the Rio Grande flows for many miles and many days before it reaches us," my *papá* told me one day when we were fishing.

That was the day before my sixth birthday, but because I had never been more than a few miles away from the ranch where we lived, I didn't know much about distances. I did know that for as long as I could remember, I had always wanted to go to San Antonio, which *Papá* always described as being "about five hours directly north."

My father went to San Antonio every year on the first Sunday in September to sell the watermelons he and my mother had raised on the little piece of land behind our home.

Every year my father would say: "When you're a little older, like six or seven, Pedrito, you will go with me to San Antonio. You will help me sell the *sandías*."

I lived with my father, my mother, and my three-year-old sister María Elena, whom we called Elenita, near the river in a small one-room house on the farm where my father worked. My father was the farm's only employee, an all-around handyman who fed the animals, planted the crops, milked the cows, and managed whatever else had to be done. The farm was called *La Noche Buena;* after all, my father explained, the owners bought the property on Christmas Eve. Behind our hut, my father and mother raised a few vegetables, a few chickens, a couple of goats, and a hog or two. There was also our *burro,* which spent hours tied to a mesquite tree, chewing on whatever you gave him, never complaining.

Our *burrito* was especially useful that summer before my sixth birthday. It had been very hot and we hadn't had any rain since the winter before. Every day, as I played outside, my mother would summon me, "*Hijito,* let's go to the river." So we placed two vats on the *burro* and my mother, my sister, and I would go to the river to bring back water for our watermelons.

One evening, as we enjoyed our supper of tamales and refried beans, my father turned to me and said, "Pedrito, you and I are going to San Antonio tomorrow. Happy birthday." I ran around the little table, my eyes full of tears of joy, and hugged my father.

My dream was coming true. My mother also cried, and Elenita only wanted to know "*¿Qué pasa?*" but no one was listening to her.

"*Sí,* Pedrito, tomorrow morning, *hijito,* we're getting up very early. We will fill the old pickup with watermelons and take them to the market in San Antonio.

"You were very good this summer, *hijito.* I could see you helping your mother remove the weeds from the watermelon patch. And you're carrying water from the river. That's a big man's job, my son." I could only beam with delight.

I had spent lots of time near those watermelons. "What are you doing to those watermelons, *hijito?*" asked my mother when she caught me in the patch. "It's too hot, Pedrito. Come get in the shade." It was always too hot, particularly that July and August. But here we were in early September and it wasn't much cooler. There really wasn't much to protect us from the sun. The few mesquite trees around our house were short and their leaves were thin. The cactus didn't grow very high and didn't help, either.

Sunday, my father said, was a good market day in San Antonio. The few chores he did on Sunday, such as milking the cows and feeding the animals, my mother could handle. She worked alongside my father frequently and could do any of his chores.

"You're a big boy now," my father said. "You will help me haul the watermelons to market. Maybe even help me sell them," he said, with a wink in his eye. "Next week you'll be going to school. We'll need a little extra money to buy you some of those school supplies. Maybe a pencil and a tablet, also. Maybe some crayons," he added. "And who knows? If we make enough, maybe even a lunch box. Would you like that?" he asked, drawing a box on the hot sand.

"*Sí, Papá,*" I said. We both laughed at the thought of a lunch box.

I laughed but I was nervous. Never having been to school before, I wasn't sure I was ready for the experience. I accepted the fact that my parents insisted I must attend school. "Just like all the other Mexican kids in all the ranches around us," my mother said.

Before the sun was up the following morning, my father woke me and told me to get ready for our trip. He didn't have to call me twice. I had been awake half the night. My mother, who had left my clean clothes by my side the night before, was already outdoors by the grill my father had built. She was making coffee, grilling tortillas, cooking some eggs with sausage, and fixing some refried beans. We did not have an indoor kitchen yet in our simple, little one-room house.

"One of these days," my father promised my mother, "I will build you an indoor kitchen." In the meantime, we made do with the little grill my father welded together from scrap iron, plus a few utensils collected from friends and neighbors, and two wooden boxes my father assembled to serve as places to sit and to hold all the utensils.

Sometimes at night we stored the food inside those boxes, tightly wrapped, to keep it away from the coyotes.

While my mother prepared breakfast, my father and I went to the watermelon patch and started cutting and loading them on the truck. "I'm the only one who drives this old pickup," said my father. "That's why I always keep it in top condition." The truck belonged to the owner of the farm, Mr. Shaffer, who allowed my father to use it, even for personal purposes, such as the annual trip to San Antonio and whenever we went into the village to attend church, which wasn't that often. My father sometimes said, "We have too much work to do today, even if it's Sunday." Some weeks there was no priest to celebrate the Mass, so several of the older ladies simply led the people in praying the Rosary. The one priest in the city, Father Gustavo, had to serve all the missions in the surrounding communities of the main church.

At the patch, *Papito* picked a large watermelon covered with the morning dew, dropped it on a rock, and signaled for me to dig in and enjoy some of the heart that revealed itself so red and juicy. I always enjoyed this ritual, which we repeated on many a morning, tasting to see how ripe and juicy and sweet the watermelons were. If they weren't, my father would say, "Leave it for the crows." We always saw the crows waiting on the mesquite trees, ready to attack the melons. We usually tried the melons in the morning, when it was cooler and the dew that covered them overnight gave them a refreshing taste. Once the sun began to warm the day, you couldn't touch the watermelons without feeling your fingers burn.

"These watermelons are perfectly ripe, Pedrito. Those city folk in San Antonio are going to love them," said my father as we sampled the sweet fruit.

After we had both had our fill, *Papito* said, "Leave the rest to the birds and the rabbits, Pedrito. Heaven knows there'll be plenty of them coming around. *Mamacita* still has breakfast waiting for us."

After we ate our breakfast, Mama took the leftover tortillas, folded them into *taquitos,* and filled them with the rest of the eggs, sausage, and refried beans. "So you will not hunger," she said. "It's a long trip."

She blessed us several times, *"Qué Dios les bendiga. Qué vayan con la Virgen de Guadalupe. Qué Jesús, María y José vayan con ustedes,"* she kept repeating. My father, showing some slight annoyance, said, *"Mujer,* we'll be back tonight. We're not going to the end of the world. That's enough praying. Enough with your blessings."

"There's no such thing as too much praying," said my mother. "Anyway, take care of my son—your son, our son."

He vowed to watch carefully after me. And off we went to San Antonio.

About an hour after we had been driving north, we came upon a police car with flashing lights by the edge of the highway. Two men in uniform signaled for us to stop.

*"¿Qué es, Papá?"* I said, trembling, for I sensed something was wrong by the way my father squinted his eyes, stared, and bit his lips.

*"Nada, hijito,"* he said. "It's only the Border Patrol checking for illegal Mexicans. I have my working papers, so there's nothing to worry about."

As we pulled up alongside the officers, one of them asked my father in Spanish and in English, *"¿Qué llevas?* What are you carrying?"

"Can't they see we're carrying watermelons," I thought to myself, although they were partly covered with a large serape to protect them from the hot sun. *"Sandías.* Watermelons," my father, who had learned a few words of English, answered in Spanish and in English.

*"¿Adonde?* Where to?"

*"A San Antonio. A la marqueta,"* said my father.

"What are you carrying under the watermelons?" asked one of the officers.

*"Nada,"* said my father. *"No, sólo sandías."*

"Well," said the other officer, "you better start unloading them. After all, you never know what you might find under a wetback's *sandías*, eh, Joe?"

The one called Joe nodded, saying, "Like marijuana. Or tequila."

So my father and I unloaded all the *sandías*. I climbed on the truck and handed my father one *sandía* at a time. I was sweating from the heat and from fear, and the watermelons were very heavy, but I kept on handing my father one at a time. We didn't say a word. I think we both feared that the officers would get mad. I was mad and confused, and every time one of them put his hand on his gun, dozens of thoughts raced through my mind: "Will they shoot us? Will they send us back home? Will I ever get to see San Antonio? Will they keep all our watermelons?" My father remained expressionless. He didn't even whistle, which he often did while he worked.

As we unloaded, the officers sat in the shade of the mesquite trees a few feet from us, drinking cold water out of canteens, making me feel very thirsty. "I wish I was back home," I thought. "No," I'd reconsider, "I must see San Antonio."

There were only two watermelons left on the truck before the officers were satisfied. By the time we finished we were completely wet with sweat—both because it was so horribly hot and because we were so nervous.

"OK, load up and get out of here," said the officer called Joe.

"Oh, and never let me catch you with a load of marijuana. I'll cut you and your son up into a hundred pieces if I ever do," the other one said, laughing loudly.

They both laughed again and threw friendly punches at one another. My father didn't seem to find it very funny. I know I didn't, although I didn't really understand much of what was going on. I wanted to cry but I knew I had to be strong, as my father and mother had always taught me.

As we reloaded our sixty *sandías,* the meaner of the two officers said, "I'll take that one," and, pointing to another one, "and my partner wants that one, for all our troubles." They again laughed loudly, having taken our two largest melons.

But my father wasn't laughing. I could tell he was mad, but there was nothing we could do. We simply rode away and I began to cry.

"No, Pedrito, you're a big boy now. You have to be strong. You cannot let bad people ruin your life. What's two watermelons? If we sell all the rest of them, and I think we will because they look so beautiful, we'll make a nice profit. Oh, a little down the road we'll stop and I'll buy you a soda or some lemonade," he said. I could hardly wait.

"I'm very afraid, *Jefe,*" I said. We sometimes called him *Jefe* or *Jefecito* because he was the boss, even though my father said my mother was the real *jefecita.*

"You can't really blame the officers," my father added. "There are bad people who bring drugs in from Mexico, and because of a few rotten people, they suspect everyone. They seem to think that all Mexicans are liars and thieves and that they bring illegal drugs and tequila into the country."

"But they don't have to be so mean about it, *Papito,*" I said.

We drove on without either of us saying another word, except when my father said, making the sign of the cross, "By noon, God willing."

By eleven o'clock, we saw a little settlement with a gas station and a restaurant. We slowed down and we were about to pull into the restaurant when my father struggled to read a sign by the door of the restaurant. It took him a long time, for he could hardly read, his lips moving but not making any sounds.

"*¿Qué es, Papito?*" I said, for I still didn't know how to read, never having attended a day of school before. My father, who hardly had gone to school himself, hesitated, then read slowly, practically forming each letter at a time, "No niggers. No Mexicans. No dogs."

"What does that mean, *Papito?*"

"It means we are not allowed to enter that restaurant, *hijito*. I need some gas for the truck, but I can go a little farther. I will not give them my business if they can't even give us a glass of water to drink."

"Why, *Papito?*"

"Remember, Pedrito, I told you there are evil people in this world? These people are evil. Thank God most of the people we know are good. We'll soon find another place and I'll buy you a nice big soda. And one for myself, *niño.* We'll fill up our gas tank. And we'll be off to beautiful San Antonio."

A few minutes later we saw another settlement. This one had a crude sign out, "Mexican Food," which my father understood immediately, to our relief. We stopped and bought two cold sodas. The lady who served us, probably noticing I was covered with sweat, said, "*Agua para el niño,* water for the boy," and handed me a large glass of cold water, colder and better tasting than I had ever had before. We had no ice at our ranch to make cold water, and somehow the water we got from the Rio Grande didn't taste as good as this, which my father said came from a well.

We drank our sodas as the truck was being filled up with gas. With my soda in hand, the restaurant that wouldn't serve us and those nasty officers suddenly seemed far behind, at least in my mind. So off we went to San Antonio, laughing and singing until we saw the outskirts of the city. My eyes were as big as the watermelons. My mouth was as wide as a full moon.

We were so happy, forgetting the bad part of our trip, as we drove into the city and sang one of our favorite songs at the top of our voices, all the way to the market:

*"Allá en el rancho grande, allá donde vivía*
*Había una rancherita, que alegre me decía, que alegre me decía.*
*¿Qué te decía, hombre? . . ."*

# Chapter 2

## Sweet Home, Sweet Watermelons

My father, José, was born on a tenant farm just south of the Rio Grande in northern Mexico, the oldest of seven children. When he was my age, he attended a country school for two years where he barely learned how to read and write. But after two years, with brothers and sisters arriving fast and very little food or money in the house, he was forced to work in the fields, picking cotton, onions, peppers, corn, carrots, whatever was in season. In this warm climate, the season seemed to last all year. The only times the pickings were meager were during extremely dry seasons.

When my father was fourteen, his father called him outside, and the two talked to his uncle Jesús—his father's older brother—who worked for a vegetable and fruit farmer across the river, in the Rio Grande Valley of Texas. Uncle Jesús was getting old and tired and the farmer had agreed to let him find a helper. If the helper was any good, he could take over for Jesús when Jesús decided to retire. But this would not be for several years, Jesús had assured the farmer, Mr. Shaffer.

"Times are bad in Texas and the pay is poor," said *Tío* Jesús, whom my grandfather usually called by his nickname, Chucho.

"But they are worse here in Mexico," said the father to his son. "You won't be that far away. It's less than an hour's walk from here across the river."

"*Sí, Papá,* I will go with *Tío* Jesús," said José, accepting the fact that there really was no choice. This would mean one less mouth to feed for his parents, and perhaps José could send home a few pennies from time to time to help the family survive.

In the middle of the night, José and his uncle left for the river, accompanied by José's father. His mother simply kissed him good-bye and gave him her blessings, holding back tears, not wanting to follow them to the river and prolong her agony of seeing her firstborn leave home for work. José's father hugged his son and his brother and waved them off at the crossing, an area where the water was shallow, a desertlike area not likely to be covered by the Border Patrol.

When they were safely on the other side, they whistled a predetermined long and short sound so the father would know they had made it safely into Texas. The next day José began learning all the tasks of the farm: planting and harvesting the crops, driving the tractor and the truck, milking the cows, tending to the hogs. "I was so small, I needed two pillows to see over the steering wheel," he told me many years later as he recalled his early days on the farm.

He lived in a tiny shack at the northern edge of the farm with his uncle Jesús, the same house where I was born several years later and where my family lived for many years. Jesús had never married and had no family other than his brothers, sisters, nephews, and nieces in Mexico. José sometimes felt that his uncle was very lonely and that all he had was his work. José vowed that if he were to remain in Texas, he would one day return to Mexico, get married, and bring back a bride.

The years passed and José worked along with his uncle, Mr.

Shaffer, and Mr. Shaffer's son, Jerry. He learned much of his English from Jerry, who was a couple of years older and was expected to one day take over the farm from his father. José also taught Jerry some Spanish. "When I take over the farm, José, do you want to work for me?" Jerry often asked José.

José would laugh. *"Pues sí, amigo,"* he said, not sure that was what he wanted to do the rest of his life, like his uncle. But was there anything else? He really liked Jerry, and Jerry was always nice to him. Over the next few years, my father worked hard and every day felt more confident of one day taking over the farm from his Uncle Chucho.

In 1932, when José was twenty, his uncle complained of heavy pains in his stomach over a period of several days. "Walk with me to the river tonight," *Tío* Jesús told José one day. "I already told Mr. Shaffer. I need to go home"—Mexico was always home, no matter how long we had been away—"and see if someone will fix me some tea for this stomachache that won't go away."

The river was crested that evening after unusually heavy rains upstream, and the water current was running heavy. But *Tío* Chucho insisted on returning to Mexico, for he feared he was too sick to remain behind. He had crossed the Rio Grande dozens of times and had no fear, but this time he was sick and weak from all the pain. Because of the darkness, the high and choppy water, and the howling wolves, my father never heard his uncle give the usual signal, a long and then a short, loud whistle. He had no idea whether his uncle had made it home. The following day, Mr. Shaffer called my father into his house. "They found your uncle's body a couple of miles down the river," he told my father. "The sheriff's office came by and said he carried papers identifying him as being from my farm. He was a good man, a good worker," said Mr. Shaffer. "I will miss him."

My father says he detected a tear in Mr. Shaffer's eye, but Mr. Shaffer turned away and told him to notify his people. Mr. Shaffer arranged for the sheriff's office to place Uncle Chucho in a coffin, and two of my father's neighbors helped to carry the coffin across the river. There they were met by my grandfather and his brothers, who would bury their beloved brother on the family farm.

"You're now in charge," Mr. Shaffer told José the following day. "You know what to do." My father nodded, as Mr. Shaffer continued: "I'm proud to have you. You're a good worker. You'll do *muy bien,*" he said in his broken Spanish.

José enjoyed the work and the fact that he could send some money home to help the rest of the family. But after a year he felt very lonely and longed for a bride. On a visit home, he told his parents of his wishes. His parents agreed he should be married, and his father said, "You know that pretty girl down the road, Don Damian's daughter María Guadalupe?"

"Yes, *Papá.* I've seen her by the river several times, washing clothes or hauling water. She's really grown up now. And a very pretty girl she is, too."

"I think she would be a perfect wife for you. Nice, hardworking family. I think she's about eighteen and should be ready for marriage. I will ask Don Damian," said his father.

José returned to his job in Texas, hoping Don Damian would agree to give his daughter to José in marriage. Fifteen days had passed with no answer from Don Damian. José's father sent word with someone sneaking across the river into Texas.

"Don't worry. This is good news," the messenger said, quoting José's father. "Custom dictates that if the parents don't say no to the match in fifteen days, they will say yes in a month."

And so it was. José and María Guadalupe, who had hardly ever spoken to one another, became bride and groom in the tiny chapel near their ranch in Mexico where a priest visited once or twice a year to celebrate Mass, hear confessions, perform baptisms, and preside at weddings.

That night the newlyweds swam back to the Texas ranch with the bride's few belongings in one large potato sack and a few gifts in another. They tried to hold the sacks over their heads to keep them dry.

In that little shack my granduncle had built, I was born in 1935. Three years later, my sister María Elena arrived.


We sold all our watermelons in San Antonio by midafternoon. Anyone who opened one and saw how ripe and juicy it was, could not resist buying a second one. "*Ay, qué dulce.* Oh, how sweet," said one woman. "One for me, one for my neighbor," said an elderly lady.

There were dozens of vendors up and down the large open marketplace. Everything was for sale, from shoes to clothes to vegetables and fruits.

One merchant bought one of our watermelons, and we bought some of her lemonade to go with the *taquitos* my mother had packed for us.

She had been watching me as I picked up watermelons or offered to cut one open for anyone wanting a taste. "*Ay, qué niño tan guapo,* what a smart, hardworking boy," she told me, making sure my proud father heard her. I too was very proud of myself, as another woman said, "So young, and so energetic. I wish my teenagers were half as good."

It was late afternoon and there was only one watermelon left. My father cut it up, called out to a group of boys hanging around the market, and handed each a piece. They each grabbed their piece of watermelon and ran.

"Why are they running?" I asked.

"They're afraid I'm going to make them pay for the melon or put them to work," my father said.

*"Pobrecitos,"* said my father. "Poor kids. They are like little animals. Abandoned by their parents. They live in the streets and off the streets. Some as young as you, Pedrito. What's to become of them?"

I was too shocked to say anything. For years to come, I could never forget those hungry eyes, those nervous looks.

It was time to say good-bye to some of the other vendors we had met that day and to head for home. *"Hasta el año que viene,"* we told them all, hoping to see them again next year. I slept most of the way home and dreamed about school, which I would be attending the next day. When I fell asleep fearing what school would be like, I had bad dreams.

My father woke me up. It was suddenly dark. "What were you dreaming about, Pedrito?" he asked, adding, "You were saying, *'No, no quiero ir.'"* Yes, in my dreams I feared that unknown school and a part of me said, "No, I don't want to go." But sometimes I convinced myself that my parents were right, school would be good for me and for all the family.

My mother said she hoped that I would teach her everything I learned, for she could neither write nor read, in English or in Spanish. She had to work in the fields from the time she was six years old and never could go to school. The only school near the ranch where she was born and reared was too far away and difficult to reach. Traditionally, only boys went to school in those days, and only for a couple of years. Many of those years her family followed the crops and worked wherever they could find it. The entire family had to work the fields.

"With this money we made today, Pedrito, we should be able to buy some pencils and a notebook for you to take to school," my father said. We would buy these items the next morning at the *marqueta* near our home. The market sold everything to the farm families and their workers. "If we don't have it, we'll get it," my father quoted the owner as saying. It was to this market that I would walk each morning, with other kids from the *ranchos* all along the road to the river, to take the bus to school.

"I will be working tomorrow," said my father, "but your mother and María Elena will walk you to *la marqueta*. I wish I could go to school, too."

"Why don't you go in my place, *Papá?* I'm afraid," I said, hesitating, as we drove along and got closer to home. "Do I really have to go? Can't I wait until I'm a little older?"

"It's very important that you learn English, Pedrito. I only know a few words, what I picked up at the farm. Maybe someday you will teach me what you learn. But you can't teach me until you learn it. OK, *hijito?*"

My father sometimes called me *hijito*, "my little son," and sometimes Pedrito, or "little Pedro." I called him *Papá, Papacito, Papito,* or even *Jefe,* depending on how I felt.

My mother greeted us and crossed herself several times, inquiring over and over how we had done in San Antonio. We assured her everything had gone well. "No, the truck didn't break down either," said my father about my mother's worst fears.

"We are so blessed. So rich. So happy," my mother said as she began to fix us some tacos. Then she sat by us and began to say the Rosary, as she did silently almost every night of her life.

"*Sí, querida,* we are very lucky," my father finally answered. "We work hard but we have enough food for us and our children. What else could we ask for?"

"Well," she said, laughing and hugging me at the same time. "Soon we can start to learn English from our son, the scholar."

# Chapter 3

## "Miss, I Want to Go Out!"

"You must get a good night's rest, for tomorrow you start school," my mother said shortly after dinner. So I went to bed early but couldn't sleep. The coyotes were howling as I had never heard them before. The night seemed hotter than ever, and I sweated all night. It seemed even the roosters started crowing earlier than usual. Even when my father and I slept outside because of the heat, I don't ever remember so much howling or crowing. "I don't really want to go to school," I told myself. But then I could hear one or another of my parents saying, "Pedrito, you must go to school." I wondered in the night whether one could learn without going to school.

I really didn't understand what school was all about, and while I didn't have the answers, I didn't even know what questions to ask. With all my doubts, I always returned to the wishes of my parents. They wanted me in school. They wanted me to learn to read and writ in English and in Spanish. This was very important to them. And they wanted me to teach them everything I learned, day by day. One question never occurred to anyone but me: What if I didn't learn anything?

On that first morning, my mother and Elenita walked me to the general store, *la marqueta,* where we were to catch the bus to school. On the way we met other children and parents from the farms along the road as they too headed for the bus stop. There were about a dozen small, family-operated farms up and down the main road. Mexicans worked in most of them, and their children were all going to my school.

"*Hola,* Alicia," said my mother to a woman who joined us on our walk. "*Hola,* Juanito. . . . *Hola,* María. . . . *Buenos días,* Maruca." There were *holas* and *buenos días* all around. Alicia, whose husband worked on the farm across from ours, had been a friend of my mother's from their days growing up in Mexico. She was carrying her four-year-old daughter Maruca and walking her eight-year-old son Juanito to wait for the bus. Juanito and I had been friends for many years, playing in one another's yard when our mothers visited, which wasn't often enough, as far as we were concerned.

But I wasn't much in the mood for greetings. Finally I did talk to Juanito. "Do you remember your first day of school? Were you afraid, Juanito?"

"Don't worry, Pedrito, I'll watch over you. If anyone gives you any trouble, tell them you're Juanito's friend." I never even thought someone would give me trouble. My fears were deeper rooted.

We went into the store first, where my mother bought me a pencil and a notebook. "This is the notebook *el niño* will need in the first grade," said the store owner's wife to my mother. My mother handed the pencil and notebook to me and made me promise to keep them clean and not to lose them. I placed them both in the bag my mother had given me with my sandwich—a tortilla filled with eggs and beans—for lunch.

There were sixteen children, in various grades, taking the bus to school, which was in Rio Grande City. "It's only five miles away," one of the parents told my mother, adding, "They'll be there in half an hour, by the time we get back home." One of the boys and one of the girls on the bus were Anglos whose parents owned farms near *La Marqueta*. The rest of us were all Mexican children, the children of the farm workers.

"*Qué Dios te bendiga,*" my mother said to me when the bus arrived. I had to be brave, and I didn't dare to cry in front of the other children. I found it very difficult to hold back the tears, especially when I saw another little boy crying, kicking and refusing to get on the bus and telling his mother, "I don't want to go to school. I don't want to learn." But his mother forced him on board as the bus driver quickly closed the door behind him and ordered him to sit down. I understood his pain, first time away from his parents, like me. No idea what he was facing. The bus driver, Don Manuel, was a very kind man. He reminded me of my own grandfather, however little I ever saw him. He made sure all the children were seated, and he stopped the bus at the least sign of misbehavior.

I could see my mother still standing in front of *la marqueta* when the bus pulled away. I could see tears but also a big smile on her face. There was no going back for me.

The little boy who had been crying looked sad, but as soon as he could no longer see his mother, his tears stopped. He sat next to me and told me his name was Roel. Although he lived near me, I had never seen him before. He too was going into the first grade. I told him we would be together and that I would help him if he needed anything. He said his parents had just moved to Texas from Mexico so he could attend American schools and learn English. By his standards, I was an old-timer. I had even been to San Antonio. Suddenly I felt protective of him and forgot about my own fears.

On the way to school, one of the fourth graders said to me, "You better not use Spanish anywhere on the school grounds."

"No," warned a third grader. "If you do, the principal will take you to the bathroom and will make you wash your mouth with lye."

"That's true," added the fourth grader. "And the lye burns your mouth and you won't be able to eat or talk for three days. That's so you'll never forget and never use Spanish in the school again."

"*¿Por qué?,*" I asked. "Why can't you speak Spanish?"

"So you can learn English, dummy," volunteered the third grader, in Spanish. But she added quickly in English, "I speak only English!" Sensing I didn't know what she was saying, she repeated it in Spanish, adding "I even speak only English at home! I have no problems. My parents understand English. My teacher last year said I'm a very smart little girl. I think so too. And so do my parents."

I was terrified. I didn't know a word of English. How was I going to start speaking it automatically on the first day of school? I had to think of something to avoid having my mouth rinsed with lye.

Juanito wasn't saying much. But he moved closer to me and the other two first graders on the bus and told us not to worry. "Those kids are just trying to scare you," he whispered. He then tried to teach me and Roel, the boy who had been crying, a few important words and phrases. "Repeat after me," said Juanito, in Spanish: "Miss, I want to go out."

"*¿Qué es* 'Miss' *y todo eso,* Juanito?" I asked.

"In case you have to go to the bathroom, *niños,* you must say 'Miss, I want to go out,'" he explained.

"If you learn nothing else, you must learn these words, or you'll pee in your pants," said one of the little girls. Everyone laughed.

"When we get to school, I'll show you all where the bathrooms are," Juanito said.

We repeated "Miss, I want to go out" over and over, but by the time I got to class, nervous as I was, I forgot how to say it. Luckily, I didn't have to go out that day.

Luckily, too, the teacher didn't expect us to start speaking English immediately.

Our teacher, Miss García, met us at the bus stop and asked, in Spanish, that all six-year-olds follow her into the school. She was a very beautiful lady, tall for a Mexican, very fair-skinned, with a beautiful smile. She led us into a large room, one of four in the first of two floors of the stark-looking brick building, situated on top of a hill. The room across from us, I later learned, was for first graders who knew some English, or were the children of English-speaking parents, or had attended preschool.

Once inside our room, Miss García spoke in Spanish but warned us about using it in class.

"From now on, we will speak only English," she said. "Only in an emergency, like, 'Run, there's a fire,' will I speak to you in Spanish. We are here to learn English."

So for the first few days I avoided saying anything, in English or Spanish, unless Miss García pointed to me directly and prompted me to repeat after her.

"Red," she said. "Red," I said, as she pointed to one of the three colors on the flag.

"American flag," she said, pointing with her long ruler.

All day long we kept on repeating colors and "yes" and "no." "No" was very simple for all of us. I wished that more words in English were the same as in Spanish. Why couldn't there be only one language? Why did there have to be two? Were there other languages, or did everyone speak either English or Spanish? I wasn't sure.

Midmorning on the first day, we went outdoors and played and ran for a while. It was hot and the ground was full of little rocks. No grass and only four mesquite trees, at each corner of the school grounds. I sweated, as did most of the other children, but I was careful to keep my clothes clean. I must wear them at least two days, for my mother couldn't wash them every day and I had very few clothes to wear to school.

At noon, Miss García marched us to the boys and girls bathrooms, then told us to make sure to wash our hands by demonstrating with her own hands and saying, "Wash hands." We returned to our room, took out our lunches, and ate at our desks. After lunch, our teacher told us to put our heads down and rest. I think she was tired of repeating the colors over and over and over. And she wanted to eat her own lunch. I was glad when the day was over, happy to see it hadn't been as scary as I had feared, and excited when I finally climbed the bus for my trip back home.

When my mother and sister met me at *la marqueta,* there were kisses and hugs and my mother wanted to know what I had learned on my first day. Juanito ran ahead of us, waving good-bye. "I must run home to feed my lambs," he said, always talking about the lambs he and his family were raising.

As he left, my mother repeated, "And what did you learn in school today, Pedrito?" I said, loudly, "Red. White. Blue."

"What is that?" my poor mother wanted to know, as we walked home.

I explained, in Spanish, that those were the three colors of the American flag. "Red is *rojo,* blue is *azul,* and white is *blanco,*" I said proudly.

"The Mexican flag is red, white, and green," she said, in Spanish, but we had no idea what *green* was in English. I promised to ask Miss García the next day. Oh, but I couldn't ask her in Spanish. I must figure out something.

That night, as we enjoyed our dinner, my father and mother practiced saying the colors with me. Even Elenita joined in. It was a ritual that would continue for the rest of the school year, with me practicing every new word I learned and trying to teach and practice the word with my parents and sister.

I even taught them, "Miss, I want to go out," which I suddenly recalled as we were having dinner. The three of them enjoyed saying it, with difficulty. Miss García said it so much more clearly, I thought. I wanted to laugh at their pronunciation, but didn't.

On the second day of school I was still curious about the word for green, as in the Mexican flag. Since Miss García frequently called on me to answer her questions, I would try to figure out how to say *green* in English during one of our conversations. I found a piece of paper with green on it. As she pointed out the red, white, and blue on the flag, I repeated the colors correctly. "Good, Pedrito. Very good," she repeated.

Then I walked to the board and pointed to the color green and affected a quizzical look on my face. She understood, and said aloud, "Green."

"Green," I repeated. She laughed, as did all the children. "Green," I said again, and we had all learned another color on our second day of school. I kept repeating "green" silently in my head, for I mustn't forget. I must be able to tell my parents. I wanted to explain to Miss García that the Mexican flag had the color green, but I didn't know how. Maybe some other day.

I never forgot those four colors, and neither did the rest of my family, even little sister María Elena.

"Imagine," said my father, "when María Elena goes to school she will already know the colors. Even green."

On that second day of school, the teacher asked us to stand up, put our right hand on our hearts, and face the flag as she recited, "I pledge allegiance to the flag of the United States of America . . ." She was very good at getting us to stand or sit or face in one direction mostly through her motions, always keeping tight control of the twenty children in our class. But it was many months before we could repeat the Pledge of Allegiance along with her.

We also spent lots of time that first week of school learning the first ten numbers. One. Two. Three. Four. Midweek, we started to sing the ABCs. I found those harder to understand and to say than the numbers. But for some of the children, it was the other way around. Sadly, some had lots of difficulty with both.

I was very shy and even when Miss García said, "Sing out, Pedrito," I had difficulty. But little by little, I would sing along with some of the other kids, who seemed to have learned to sing the ABCs at home. "ABCDEFG, HIJKLMNOP . . ." Singing them made them easier to learn.

Still, it was too much to learn all at once. And there was no one to help me at home. My father knew a few words, but his pronunciation was different from the teacher's, and I sometimes had difficulty understanding him. Sometimes I would practice with Juanito and some of the older children on the bus, but the older kids were practicing their own lessons and words. I also hated to interrupt. Juanito, who usually sat in the back of the bus with the older kids, was always willing to help. He would walk to the front of the bus when he heard us younger kids grasping for the right word or pronunciation. He would also help me sometimes as we walked home from school. With Juanito along, my mother didn't show up at *la marqueta* to pick me up too often. If she needed something from *la marqueta,* she would time it to the arrival of the bus, but usually I walked with Juanito. "You need to spend time with your friend Juanito," she said, explaining why she didn't meet me at the bus stop every day after school.

I didn't mind. I enjoyed walking with Juanito, who would talk about his lambs and about taking them to the water hole near his home every afternoon and about the sad times, when his parents would butcher one of them to serve for dinner.

Over the next few weeks in school, I learned all the ABCs and one, two, threes and found it lots of fun to put numbers together, especially when it got to something like seven and nine to form a seventy-nine.

"You must learn your numbers and your ABCs," Miss García said. "The rest comes later." I began to understand what she was talking about, and soon I would be putting this to use in sentences. I was very proud of myself for all I was learning, and my parents were even prouder, or so they were constantly stating. But I didn't think they realized how much I was learning. Did they really understand what I was learning or did they simply know that it was very important for me to learn to read and write and understand English?

The fact that they wanted me to go to school was a step in the right direction, since many other parents thought it was more important to have their kids work in the fields, where they could learn to do everything useful—plant the seeds, turn on the irrigation water, and pick the vegetables and the cotton. This is what they were meant to do for the rest of their lives, right? So why go to school where they don't teach you these tasks?

I heard one man tell my father, "They're not going to teach Pedrito how to pick cotton or hoe the fields in school, *hombre*. That he has to learn in the farm, from you. Why are you sending him to school?"

"So he can learn the things I can't teach him, like how to read and write, *compadre*," said my father. "I can teach him to pick cotton or work the fields on weekends and in the summertime. Hopefully, he'll never have to do it. Maybe he'll be a teacher when he grows old."

But the *compadre* shook his head. "Teacher!" As he walked away I could hear him mumbling, "How are you gonna turn a Mexican into a teacher? A Mexican can only be a Mexican."

Maybe he's right. How do you turn a Mexican into a teacher? But wait, Miss García was Mexican, although she looked very proper and dignified. She dressed better and looked better than the Mexican mothers in our farms, who wore old jeans or homemade dresses or dresses discarded by someone else. Somehow, I couldn't imagine Miss García growing up picking cotton or working the fields.

Even if the compadre was right, I didn't care. So what if I never became a teacher? All I wanted now was to help my father and my mother. I wanted to make them happy knowing that I was learning English. I was happy with the knowledge I was gaining, if slowly and very little at a time. Even if you never use everything you learn, and you will, my father often reminded me, it never hurts. "You know how to pick cotton," he said, adding, "Maybe you'll be able to do something else too. Maybe you'll be able to read books in your spare time."

My little sister María Elena was quickly learning everything I taught her: the alphabet, the numbers, the colors of the flag. She picked these up faster than my parents. And her pronunciation was even better. Maybe when she's six years old and ready to go to school, she will be placed in Room One, with the English-speaking children, I told her. But after hearing me speak about Miss García all the time, she said, "No, I won't go to Room One. I want to be with Miss García."

"Repeat after me, María Elena," I encouraged her. "One. Two. Three. Red. White. Blue. Green."

Learning became her favorite game. While skipping rope or running around the yard, she would constantly repeat the numbers or the colors or the ABCs. She would shout out, "Miss, I want to go out!" You could see happiness written all over her face.

My parents were also happy with the results. "You're a good teacher, Juanito," said my father. "Maybe someday you will teach the numbers and the ABCs to many, many other children."

# Chapter 4

## The Great Mexican Hope

I was probably about three years old, on a trip with my mother to *la marqueta,* when I discovered the radio.

"*¿Qué es eso?*" I asked my *mamacita,* wondering what in the world was that wooden box about my height from which a strange voice, with music in the background, was coming.

Before my mother could answer, the owner of *La Marqueta* said, "*Es un radio, niño.*" It's a radio.

"And where is the man talking? Inside the box?" I asked.

"No, *niño.* You see that wire behind the radio, running outside?"

"Yes," I nodded.

"Well, it connects to the large antenna on top of the roof, and that connects us to the rest of the world. Someone says something anywhere in the world, like in China, and you hear it here almost immediately."

I had never heard about China, but I was totally fascinated with that talking box. I stood by this radio until my mother finished shopping, and on the way home I asked her, "Will we have a radio someday, *Mamá,* or is it something that only *la marqueta* has?"

"No, *hijito,* there are many radios. But they are expensive. Also they only run on electricity."

"Will we ever have electricity? Will I ever be able to talk on the radio, like the man from China?"

"Of course, Pedrito. You may not be able to talk on the radio like the man from China, but one of these days we will have a radio. Your father wants to connect the electric wires to our house, but the lines are very far away. First we have to bring in the water. Then electricity. Pedrito, you ask too many questions."

I realized as I grew older that when I asked questions that were difficult for my mother or father to answer, they would always say, "Pedrito, you ask too many questions." In retrospect, I think sometimes my questions were painful for my parents. Other times, they probably didn't know the answers, but hated to admit it.

I spoke no more, but I never forgot the radio, and every time I joined my father or my mother on a trip to *la marqueta,* I always stood by the radio and listened. I was fascinated that the music and talking were always in Spanish.

Now that I was learning English in school, I asked my father: "Do people who only understand English listen to the radio?"

"*Sí, niño,*" said my father. "You turn those buttons and you can find a station in English. Here at *la marqueta* they only listen to it in Spanish."

Over the years, the radio became my main attraction at *la marqueta.* Even when my father or mother handed me a penny or two for candy or a nickel for a soda, I quickly bought my candy or soda and returned to the side of the radio. Sometimes you could hardly hear or understand what was being said because of the static and the store owner would explain, "It's the weather. Maybe I need a bigger antenna on top of *la marqueta.*"

On our way to San Antonio the day before my birthday, my

father mentioned that he had heard a world championship fight on the radio at *la marqueta* that summer and that another one was coming up.

"Joe Louis is the boxing champion of the world," he said, as he explained to me the interest and importance of sports. "He is a black man, with skin darker than ours, Pedrito. Some people think that the darker the skin the lesser the man. I don't think that way. And neither should you.

"On the night of the next fight, I will take you to *la marqueta* and you too can listen to the fight."

"Why are they fighting?" I wanted to know.

"No, it's not like fighting your enemy or because you're mad at someone," said my father. "They fight because it's a sport, a competition. It's a skill, to see who is stronger and can throw the most punches."

I still wasn't convinced that boxing was not fighting. "What if you get hit in the nose and get a nosebleed?"

"That's possible, and it happens," said my father. "But it's part of the game."

I was totally puzzled but nevertheless, on a late September evening, my father and I walked to *la marqueta* where we found several men, including most of the workers we knew from surrounding farms, huddled around the radio. The announcer was explaining, in Spanish, that this might be the last fight for Joe Louis. He had barely won the last two fights and he might also have to join the army soon.

As the bell sounded, all the men started to whistle, shout, and applaud. The men were particularly happy when the announcer said that Louis had landed a heavy blow on the opponent, or that it appeared that Louis had just won another round.

The men talked to one another between the rounds, marveling at Louis and his powerful punches. I asked my father if the fight was in Spanish or English. "They don't fight in a specific language," said my father. "There are many radio announcers at the arena, interpreting each round in their own language for the entire world to hear."

"Nice to see a man of color as the world champion," said an elderly man. "Maybe one day we will have a Mexican at the very top of the boxing world or in other sports."

"Mexicans are too small," said another. "But maybe they'll grow bigger. We used to be even smaller, according to my grandparents. But with these American diets, we're all growing bigger."

"What American diets?" said the old man. "We're still eating beans and tortillas!" Everyone in the room burst into laughter.

But the younger man ignored the remark and the laughter. "Who knows?" he said. "Maybe not in your lifetime or mine, but maybe in the lifetime of *este niño* we will have a Mexican world champion," he added, pointing at me.

"We may be small, but we're strong and hardworking," said the old man. "Maybe we can have a Mexican champion in the lighter weights."

"But that wouldn't be the same," said the younger man. "It wouldn't sound the same as when they say on the radio, 'And now, *El Mejicano*. The new heavyweight champion of the world.'"

"Louis was born poor, very poor. Had no father to speak of. But he went to the top. Goes to show you. You can do anything, no matter the color of your skin," said the young man's father.

"He's a good man. He doesn't want to hurt anyone. He really doesn't hate white men or anybody," my father was saying, to no one in particular, but loud enough for me to hear. "He just wants to be the champion, to make his race proud of him."

As each round began, you could hear all the men saying, "Shhhhh. Quiet." But they never stopped talking, hollering, whistling, and laughing as they followed the fight's announcer. They punched one another and held up their arms as if they were fighting, teasing one another and waiting for the good word, the only word they wanted to hear, that Louis had won the fight.

When the fight was over and Louis was declared the winner, everyone cheered and whistled. But they weren't too happy when the announcer said that Louis might soon have to go to war to fight for his country.

As everyone walked out of *la marqueta* to go home, the owner announced loudly, "Don't forget to buy whatever your wives asked you to bring home. Make sure you take them at least a soda or a piece of candy. Keep them happy."

"All he wants is money, but he's got to sell his goods, to pay for the radio" said my father, as we walked out with the other men, expressing our gratitude to the store owner. We walked part of the way with other men, then the last part of the road by ourselves.

"Why are the men talking about everyone having to go to war, even Joe Louis?" I asked my father as we walked in the dark, the wolves howling in the background.

"Pedrito, there are countries far away, like Germany and Japan, that want to destroy this land. It's very sad."

"Do you have to go to war?"

"No, Pedrito, only American citizens who speak good English. Even my friend, Mr. Jerry, might have to go to war to defend our country."

"Well, I'm glad you're not *Americano, Papito*. I don't want you to go to war. But why do you say they have to go to defend our country? Do you consider America or Mexico our country?"

"Pedrito, in many ways, this is our country. You and Elenita were born here, so this is your country. Who knows if I will ever go back to Mexico, maybe not until I'm a real old man. So this is my country, too."

"Is Mexico your country and my country also?"

"Yes, Pedrito. If you go back to Mexico, you will be considered Mexican because you are my son. Let's hope this war does not extend to Mexico. Mexico has lots of riches, but it doesn't seem like Germany is ready for them yet. They want the United States first. Who knows, if they take over America, Mexico could be next."

I was wondering if Mr. Shaffer would have to go to war.

"He's probably too old, but as I said, his son Jerry will surely be called."

"Will the evil people win the war?" I wanted to know.

"No, evil people eventually lose and the good people survive. But sometimes it takes many years and much suffering—burning of villages and farms, killing people—before the good man wins. So in a sense, every person loses in a war."

"When will we know?"

"You ask too many questions, Pedrito. I can't even answer them all." He was beginning to sound like my mother.

A few days later we were back at *la marqueta* to hear a speech by the president of the United States. As soon as the president began to speak, he was drowned out by another person who was translating his words into Spanish.

I couldn't really understand what the president was saying, but my father gave me a nickel to buy a soda, said he would explain it all to me later, and asked me to go outside and sit on a bench and drink my orange soda. One of my school friends, Roel, was also outside sitting on the bench, having a soda and waiting for his father. He too was clueless about what President Roosevelt was saying, which made me feel better. Roel didn't care, but I was very curious to know what this was all about. We both walked in and out of the shop to listen to the president anyway, because of our fascination with the sound coming out of a box. Like my family, Roel's family didn't have a radio or electricity either. "But one of these days we will, especially if we move into the village like my father promised," said Roel.

On the way home, my father explained that President Roosevelt had alerted the nation about the evil men who wanted to fight. He asked everyone to sacrifice and to unite against the enemy. "The president asked everyone to save money, save water, save electricity for the war effort," he said. There wasn't much our family could save, he added. "We have no money, we have no water, and we have no electricity. On the other hand, we won't miss these things, Pedrito. People who have everything will have to give up the most."

"Maybe it's good that we don't have much so we won't have to give up much," I thought. But I still didn't understand much about war, why people had to fight, and about sacrifice. But oh, how I loved that radio! That was all I wanted to discuss as we walked home hand in hand in the dark night, careful not to step in holes on the road or to attract a rattlesnake.

"*Papá*, the kids in school say that that house is haunted," I said, pointing to an old, abandoned farmhouse. "Tell me the story."

"If you promise not to be scared, I will," said my father. "Anyway, there's nothing to fear because it's still early and what happens in that house only happens at midnight."

"What happens, *Papito?*"

"Well, Pedrito, every night at midnight, a woman all dressed in white rides around the house on a headless horse. I never saw her and I really don't believe it. Some men tell me they have seen her, but that she only appears to those who believe."

I really didn't care about the woman or the headless horse. I had other things in mind.

"Tell me, *Papito*, will we have a radio one of these days?"

"Yes, Pedrito, one of these days we will have a radio. We sure will."

"And when I grow up, will I be able to talk on the radio like President Roosevelt?"

"Of course, Pedrito. Everything is possible."

There were too many things I didn't know about the radio. How is one able to talk and have people far away hear you? But I didn't want to annoy my father with any more questions. "One day I will learn all the answers," I thought. "Maybe Miss García knows. I will ask her."

# Chapter 5

## Off to the River to Do Our Laundry

In the summertime, my mother and I went to the river every Tuesday to wash our clothes. Now that I was in school, we decided to do it on Saturdays instead. We tried to go one afternoon after school, but it was starting to get dark earlier as the fall moved into winter. The water didn't seem to be as clean and the tides seemed to be higher, forcing us to do the wash farther away from our usual place. My mother also wanted to fix dinner for my father early, so he could eat the moment he came home from the farm, always hungry and usually very tired.

"I can't go to the river to do the laundry by myself, *hijito*," my mother said. It was difficult for her to load the clothes, even though we didn't have that many, and lead the donkey down the path to the river. She also had to take my little sister with her, and María Elena was too young to understand the dangers of falling in the water or getting bit by snakes.

Our routine didn't vary much from one week to the next: we hooked our small wagon, which my Uncle Jesús had built years ago, to our *burro*, Pepe; threw the bundle of dirty clothes on top; and walked to the river. I always walked in front of Pepe, holding the rope around his neck tightly so the *burro* would not run away or get distracted, although this *burro* never did run. "He's the laziest *burro* in the whole world," *Mamacita* said. *Mamá* would walk on the side, one hand on top of the laundry, the other holding María Elena. Sometimes she would have to carry María Elena, who cried that the ground was too hot and her feet were hurting. *Mamacita* would remind her, "I told you to wear your shoes." But she hated shoes, said they hurt her, and complained they were too tight. I didn't blame her. I too preferred to go barefoot, especially in the summer. Sometimes María Elena would ride the *burro* part of the way. She loved this, and I didn't mind it on the way down to the river. But coming back was a little too difficult for poor Pepe, who was getting older, and the road was a little too steep and the load too heavy as we climbed away from the river.

To keep Elenita busy, we sometimes recited the ABCs or the one, two, threes. I would tell Elenita and my *mamá*, "Repeat after me," just the way Miss García used to tell us in school. They understood.

We usually left for the river as early as we could in the morning, just after my father had left for work. By going that early, we usually found a peaceful, small inlet, about the size of our cart, with shallow, clean water right by the river. This was our favorite spot. I loved the peaceful river. In those days the water was cleaner, clean enough to drink, and it appeared wider down the river than in our area. In late afternoon, the tide would come up and the inlet would practically disappear, or at least fill up with dirty water, too dirty to wash our clothes in. Once in a while, someone would have arrived before us and our little inlet would be occupied, so we would have to search for another spot. But usually we were lucky to find it there, as if it were just waiting for us.

To do the laundry my mother would sit in the water and I would hand her one piece of clothing at a time. Then she would scrub it with her corn husks and rinse it as the waters entered and exited the inlet. We worked together this way until all our clothes were clean.

My little sister would sit and play in the sand by the bank, but we watched her carefully to make sure she didn't run to the river, for fear she would fall in. We were all fearful of drowning. We had heard too many stories of children drowning, and my father never forgot about his Uncle Jesús who had drowned in the river not too many years before and not far from where we were.

"My cousins, nine-year-old twin sisters, drowned in this area also when I was a little girl," my mother told me one day. "They found them arm-in-arm down river. I'm sure God took them to heaven immediately. They were little angels, so pure," she added.

I had never heard this story before. "Oh, no, *Mamá*. Did anybody cry?"

"Everybody," said my mother. "Even people who didn't know them." This made me doubly afraid of the river my parents sometimes called "treacherous river."

We were all distracted then when someone across the river shouted, "*¿Eres tú*, María Guadalupe?"

"*Sí*, it's me," replied my mother. It was one of her sisters, who assured us all of our family members in Mexico were fine. She was in turn assured that we were all healthy and well-fed. Our grandparents always wanted to make sure that we were "well-fed," that there was enough food, especially for the children.

Frequently, one of my mother's or father's sisters or cousins or other relatives would be doing their own laundry across the river, in Mexico, at the same time we were there, on the Texas side. So it wasn't unusual for us to communicate back and forth. Whoever was there would bring us news about our relatives, and my mother would shout back any good news in our family. She always told them how proud she was that I was in school and learning "lots of English."

"Say something in English for your *tía*," my mother encouraged me—well, actually shouted at me, not so much so I could hear her but so our relatives across the river could hear the request also. When it wasn't very windy and the river was very peaceful, you could hear people shouting across the river. Otherwise, it was difficult.

"My name is Pedrito," I would shout as loud as I could across the river, as much as I hated to do so.

*"Ay, qué guapo, qué bueno,"* I could hear them say, and everyone would laugh on both sides of the river.

But *Mamacita* would get back to her wash and scrub and scrub, using the soap she had made the winter before with lye and fat from the big pig we usually butchered every winter. She always sang as she worked, unless she was telling Elenita to stay put, or telling me to bring her something or other. One day when the water was calm, the sun not too hot, and no one around to hear us, she sang out loud, entertaining my sister and me:

*Estas son las mañanitas que pintava el Dios Señor . . .*

How beautiful she sounded and how happy she seemed. What a beautiful mother I had: black hair, light brown skin, dark eyes. Short and thin. I loved her very much and I knew that my father and my sister also did. "I love you," I told my mother as she sang. "I love you, *Mamá*," repeated Elenita. "I love you both also," said my mother, as she continued to hum her *"Mañanitas."*

"This is such a beautiful song," said my mother. "It always makes me feel so good. It's about a beautiful morning and how the good Lord created it for us to enjoy. I have always loved it. Always will. Always makes me happy. My cousins sang it at our wedding, accompanied by their guitars. Your father sang it to me on our first morning at Mr. Shaffer's ranch."

"Will we always have to come to the river to wash our clothes?" I asked my mother.

"No, Pedrito, not forever," she said. "Your *papá* says that one day Mr. Shaffer will let him put a water line between his house and ours and we will have running water."

"Our own running water!" I shouted so loud I'm sure our relatives across the river could hear me. We could bathe in it. We could drink it. We could make coffee and tea. And we would never have to go to Mr. Shaffer's well to get our drinking water, one bucket at a time.

"Of course," she shrugged, "if the well runs low, as it sometimes does, we'll still have to depend on the river for our water."

While at the river, she would wash me and my sister thoroughly. Then she would also wash herself. "Easier than at home," she said, as she washed and sang.

My *mamá* looked so happy, thinking about those days ahead when we would have water and electricity and an indoor kitchen. She smiled and closed her eyes, as if daydreaming. I looked at her and wondered if she was in another world.

The silence was suddenly broken when we heard someone coming. In the distance we could hear our old friend Doña María.

Doña María was one of those women who knew everyone in all the ranches up and down the river. She delivered babies, said prayers at funerals when the priest was not around, led the Rosary when people gathered to pray for rain, which was often, considering how little there was, and fixed special teas for all ailments, from headaches to stomachaches to colds.

*"Buen día, mujer. Buen día, niños,"* she shouted at us as she approached, carrying a bundle of her clothing.

*"¿Cómo está,* Doña María?" my mother asked.

*"Ay hija, me duele todo, pero bueno, estoy bien, gracias a Dios."* Yes, Doña María always told you she was hurting all over, raising her arms to point to all parts of her body, from top to bottom. But just as quickly, she would say, "Thank the good Lord and Our Lady of Guadalupe, I'm fine."

I think part of her problem was that she was so fat, and getting older, and this made it difficult for her to walk, but we never talked about it. I did tell my mother once, but she warned me never to say anything bad about Doña María, who was "like our savior."

I knew that with Doña María's arrival, we would be staying near the river longer. Before I could think it, my mother said, "Pedrito, let's help Doña María with her clothes. We'll stay a little longer, then we'll all walk back home together." And she began to help the old lady with her laundry.

"Poor Pepe," I thought, "now he has to carry Doña María's laundry back also."

Doña María lived near *la marqueta,* across from where we took the bus to school, so her walk to the river to do her laundry was farther than ours. She had no children and her husband was even older than she was, so she had no one to help her with her laundry. I often wondered why this woman, who had delivered so many "dozens" of children up and down the ranches of the valley, according to her count, never had any of her own. My mother would get very irritated when I asked, only explaining that "this is the way of the Lord, *niño,* and not for you to question."

Doña María told us she had been up late the night before. "You'll never guess what I was doing." she said. And without waiting for anyone to guess, she provided the answer: "What else? Delivering another baby."

She continued talking nonstop: "Baby and mother and father and everyone is fine. I did a good job, too. I always do a good job, never lost a baby. But, as usual, nobody thinks about me, only about the baby and the mother," she said. She laughed so loud at her own remarks that, again, the women across the river could hear. They all stopped washing and we could hear them laughing. While they couldn't hear the entire conversation, they probably thought there was a good joke being told on our side.

"This dear lady delivered you and your sister when you were born," my mother reminded me. She reminded me of this whenever we saw her, and Doña María would express great satisfaction, laugh loudly, and add: "And see what a good job I did? What wonderful children." I was too young to know what a good delivery had to do with children being wonderful, but I never asked. I knew that every time I asked what something meant in front of Doña María, my mother would give me that dirty look, or would tell me to run along and play and that she would explain later, but she never did explain.

We waited until Doña María finished her laundry. I was mildly irritated, though the old lady had very little laundry and, with the help of my mother, finished quickly. But my mother looked at me crossly when I showed my irritation.

"We must help one another, Pedrito."

I walked away and picked up some rocks and threw them at the river. I wanted to get home. I was getting hungry. I needed to take lunch to my father in the fields. And I wanted to practice my lessons and read the new book Miss García had lent me.

We finally started our trip home, my mother, sister, and I repeating our ABCs and one, two, threes. As we paused by the side of the road, Doña María uttered: "What beautiful English the three of you speak."

# Chapter 6

## "There Will Always Be *Curanderas*"

Doña María was a major presence in our lives. Whenever we called on her, she always came running. Usually my father would go to her home and bring her back with him. When my mother was having problems sleeping, she turned, reluctantly, to Doña María, but only after my father insisted upon it. We noticed that my mother's usual smile had disappeared from her face. She looked tired all the time. The old lady came and prepared a special tea—her specialty—and prayed with my mother every evening. The two would go inside our little house alone and pray.

"*Tanto tiempo,*" so much time, my father would say as he grew impatient when the two women remained inside the house for a long time. He and I and my sister sat outside the little house, drinking our own tea and repeating my school lessons. "Don't worry," he would say to me when I stared at him. "I'm just talking nonsense. Doña María is helping your mother. She will be fine." Sometimes my father was sure Doña María would help. Other times he wasn't so sure. But most of the time, even if he didn't believe, in his heart he wished for a cure.

After a few days, my *mamacita* was well again, to my relief and that of my father. For Elenita, life went on, not noticing my mother's illness. She played with the little doll my mother made for her. She sang "ABCDEFG . . ." to her doll, sometimes messing up the order of the letters. I guess you don't worry about a thing like that when you're only three years old. When you're six years old, like I was, you worry.

Doña María was also a great help the summer before, when our Elenita had a crying spell that lasted for hours. "Where does it hurt, *niña*," my parents repeated over and over, but they got no answer. When Mama and Papa couldn't calm her down, my father went for Doña María. She took one look at Elenita and declared: *"Ay hijos, le hicieron ojo."* That meant someone had cast an evil eye on María Elena, but not intentionally, Doña María assured us. "Perhaps seeing what a pretty girl she is, with those big beautiful brown eyes, they stared long and lovingly at her and that did it," said Doña María.

*"Ay,"* said my mother. "It must have been that man or his wife who stopped by our house to take a drink of water on their way north from Mexico. Now that I remember, it was only minutes after they left that Elenita started to cry."

"Anytime a stranger stares at her again," said the wise lady, "make sure they touch her eyes and then she will never get the evil eye again."

My father wasn't too sure that was the problem with Elenita. I could tell by his stare, that look of his when he didn't believe something. But he didn't say anything.

"Quickly, bring me an egg," Doña María said to my mother. So Doña María prayed over our little girl, holding the egg in her hand as she kept making the sign of the cross over my sister. I had difficulty holding my laughter as I looked at Doña María, this short, fat woman, her big body, always wearing a long black dress and her head covered with a black shawl, standing over the tiny girl, making the sign of the cross as she prayed. After she prayed a decade of the Rosary, which she said was required for such a cure, she broke the egg and there in the middle of the yolk she claimed she detected that "evil" eye. *"Miren,"* said Doña María, "look at the evil eye. I've removed it from Elenita." We all looked, but to me, the little white spot on the yellow of the egg didn't look much different from those of other eggs. However, Elenita stopped crying and fell soundly asleep almost immediately. She slept until the following morning, making up for lots of lost sleep.

My father uttered what I only thought. "All eggs have those little white bits that look like eyes," he laughed.

"José!" my mother said, adding loudly, "*Cállate*—shut up."

My father felt badly and said: "If Doña María says it's the evil eye and she has removed it from our Elenita and she has stopped crying, who am I to doubt it?"

I myself wasn't too sure, but I had faith in Doña María; after all, she had cured me of my severe leg pains. The year before, when the northern winds blew particularly hard and cold, my legs would hurt so much I would cry all night long. My mother would lie by my side and rub my legs to keep them warm, making them feel slightly better, but not by much. One day, my father, at the urging of my mother, went to Doña María and asked her to see if she could do anything to alleviate my pain.

Doña María said she knew exactly how to deal with my illness. She had seen the problem before in other young boys. "I will pray over him for seven days and will fix him one of my special teas—I know exactly the one—to heal his little muscles and bones. He's just growing too fast. It always happens at that age, to all my little boys. And I make them all well," she said, as she raised her head to heaven. After seven days, she assured my mother and father, the pain would disappear.

So for seven days, Doña María came by our house late in the afternoon. The two of us would go inside, and she would ask me to lie silently on the floor with my arms stretched out. She would cover me with a white sheet—"It must be white, the color of purity," she told my mother—and, holding a crucifix over my body, she would make the sign of the cross from head to toe and arm to arm. She would pray seven Our Fathers and seven Hail Marys, while I just lay there and sweated. I could sometimes hear my mother praying outside, asking the good Lord and Our Lady of Guadalupe to cure me.

*"El Padre Nuestro que estás en el Cielo . . . Ave María, Madre de Dios, ruega por nosotros los pecadores . . ."* Doña María made me repeat after her over and over. "Louder child, the Lord has to hear you. He needs to know you want to feel better."

When she was finished, she would cry out, "Pedrito, *levántate.*" Get up, Pedrito. But she warned me not to get up until she called me the third time, according to the rules of the cure. She said it so loud that I wanted to rise immediately, but waited until the third summons.

After the third day of this ritual, the pain began to disappear. I hated the tea that I had to take after each session, even with lots of sugar, but after seven days, when the pain went away and never returned, I was glad for the tea and the prayers. With those prayers I learned after hearing them over and over again, I prayed to God that I would never have such horrible pains again. More than the pain, I prayed that I would never have to put up with Doña María again.

On the last day of my cure, Doña María stopped in the middle of a prayer. A loud ripping noise and terrible *olor* filled the room. She continued with her prayer as if nothing had happened, and brought her big, heavy hands up to my forehead. I tried not to laugh but couldn't hold it. She also had to laugh. "*Ay, hijo,* I hope your parents didn't hear it. I couldn't help it. All those beans. Shhhh. Don't tell them anything." And she moved right into her prayers. *"Ave María, Madre de Dios . . ."*

One day I asked my parents if Doña María had ever gone to school, and if so, why did she not speak any English.

"Oh, no," said my father. "I don't think she ever went to school, in English or in Spanish."

"She has a gift from God," said my mother. "God placed her here to help us, to cure us and to care for us. She learned the prayers and the proper herbs and teas to use from an older *curandera,* who died years ago. It's something that's passed from one older woman to another. The *curandera* also taught her how to bring God's children into this world. Every community has a *curandera,* and when one gets too old, she seeks out a younger, wise woman and teaches her all she knows.

"Not everyone can be a *curandera.* They are gifts from God," my mother continued. "They are born with special talents. And the older *curandera* always knows whom to pick as her successor. The good Lord guides her in her selection."

"If she can't even read, how does she know what tea is good for what ailment?" I wanted to know.

"She can smell the different herbs," said my father.

"Where do the herbs come from?" I asked.

My father explained that they all grew on the ground, like our vegetables. Most of them grew on the side of the mountains between the Rio Grande and Monterrey. An older male *curandero,* whose name was Don Jaramillo, came by her house twice a year and supplied her with herbs for the various teas. He knew even more than Doña María, said my mother. He would visit all the *curanderas* in all the ranches up and down the river, selling them new supplies of special teas. He would also sell them relics and prayer cards, like the ones we bought from Doña María every time one of us got sick. We were forced to wear the relics around our neck until they fell apart. And the cards with images of Our Lady of Guadalupe my mother would pin on the wall. We had several of these because this is how we paid Doña María, by buying her cards. Not that she ever left our house without some food, especially when my mother made her favorite tamales.

My mother didn't have a sewing machine, so when she collected enough pieces of cloth, such as the ones from the flour sacks, she would take them to Doña María's house and use her sewing machine to make a shirt or a pair of underwear for me, or a dress for María Elena. We spent much time at Doña María's, and my mother would always take her some *tortillitas* or tamales. Doña María never said no to food and would usually say, "Not for me; for my poor sick husband who would die of hunger but for the kindness of all my friends." But she never hesitated to try some of the offering, right before our eyes and as soon as we arrived. *"Ay, qué lindo está,"* she would always say. She loved everything and ate everything.

"Doña María is getting old," said *Mamá.* "I wonder who will be the new *curandera?* Will we like her and will she like us? If not, who will help us?" I was curious that someone like this wise lady who could cure everyone's illness would be unable to cure her own. Well, I guess everyone has to die.

"They say the new priest in the village, Father Gustavo, is also a doctor and has better medicines that work much faster than teas," said my father. "Mr. Shaffer says he came from Germany, as did Mr. Shaffer's parents, and that the Germans know a lot about medicine and have discovered many miracle drugs. Father Gustavo also gives out drugs that he brought with him from Germany to the poor people, free of charge," he added.

"But there's no one like Doña María. She's a gift from our dear God," said my mother. "I hope someone learns her profession and follows her when she dies. I don't know what we would do without one."

"I don't want to go to the German priest if I get sick," I said. "I would be afraid of him. *Papá,* I think I like Doña María more and more every day. I will be very sad when she dies."

"Don't worry," said my father. "There will always be *curanderas.*"

# Chapter 7

## Time to Butcher Our Hog

*El Norte* arrived in the middle of the night one mid-December day. The winters were usually mild in our valley, but when *El Norte* decided to act up, as Doña María said, you went from sweating to freezing in seconds. And this was one of the worst. Pots and pans were tossed all over the yard. The poor animals were howling with fear. We donned all our clothes, huddled together trying to get warm, and covered ourselves from head to toe, for our little cabin was very cold. The wind whipped against the roof, and it sounded as if it were being torn apart.

When the winds died down a little, and the day began to dawn, my father arose and built a big fire outdoors. The week before, Miss García had shown us pictures of children playing in the snow in the north. I was fascinated with this "frozen, feathery water," as she described it. "Who knows if you'll ever see snow here. It hardly ever snows in our valley," she said.

When my father came in after building the fire, I asked him, "*Papacito,* is it snowing yet?" I had never seen it but I still wanted to experience it.

"No, Pedrito, you know it only snows once every twenty-five or thirty years here." Maybe it didn't get as cold as some of those places "up north," as Miss García said.

In preparation for the Christmas holiday, Miss García had also mounted some pictures the previous week of children playing in the snow. It really got me thinking and wondering about snow. She tried to explain to us in simple language what snow was all about. "Lots and lots of snow falls in some places," she said, acting out the snow falling with her arms and fingers. "People are forced to stay in their homes. Children can't go to school." To make sure we understood, she even said part of it in Spanish: *"Mucha nieve, mucho frío,"* she said as she shook her entire body. She hung up a painting showing a snow-covered mountain. I closed my eyes and dreamed that one day I would see a mountain covered with snow. I was willing to put up with the cold, just to see the fluffy white stuff. I wondered how long we would have to wait before snow came to our valley again.

Miss García said that where it snows, children go outdoors and hold their hands up to catch the fluffy, little feathers. She saw it once in a movie. They even make snowmen, and they throw snowballs at one another. Miss García drew a snowman on the board. The homes where these children live, she said, have large fireplaces and they build big fires inside to keep the houses warm. I couldn't imagine building fires inside the house. Wouldn't the house burn down? My father would never let us light a fire in ours. "It's too dangerous," he said.

"How cold does it get when it gets real cold, *Papito?*"

"You have to live through it, *niño*, like I did when it snowed long before you were born, maybe ten years ago. You should have seen the poor animals. They were so cold they shook all over. Several baby ducks died from the cold. I even saw some poor birds frozen in the trees. Many of the trees froze. So did many of the vegetables. We lost a lot that year. Up the valley, the orange and lemon and grapefruit trees also froze. It was three or four years before they grew fruit again."

As the winds slowed down that morning and the fire grew bigger, my mother joined my father outdoors to make some coffee and tortillas for breakfast. Elenita and I followed as soon as the tortillas were grilled.

After my father had checked and fed the animals, as the rest of us huddled around the fire, he returned and announced to my mother, "On such a clear, cool day, *querida,* let's butcher our pig." This was an annual ritual at our home around this time of year. The pig we had fed and fattened all year was ready to be turned into *chicharrones,* sausage, tamales, lard, and even soap. "Let's get started, Pedrito. You're old enough to help." As long as I could remember I would go into hiding when the pig was butchered, but my father was right, I was old enough to start helping.

First my father placed the large pot we used for our baths on the fire and filled it up with water.

"The water has to be very hot, Pedrito," he said.

My mother added, "It's to wash and shave the pig, Pedrito. You know how dirty pigs are. Once he's dead, we must wash him down thoroughly and then shave him completely. Then we'll turn his skin into *chicharrones* and the fat into lard for cooking."

When the water was almost boiling, my father, my mother, and I went into the corral and cornered the pig. While my mother and I sat on him, my father tied his legs with a rope. Mama sat on top of the hog, which was crying loud enough to be heard for miles around, and I held on to the pan to collect the blood, which Mama would turn into blood sausage later. *Papacito* picked up his sharp knife. I closed my eyes.

"*Mires,* Pedrito, you must hold the pan steady under the throat." *Papacito* blessed himself twice and then slit the pig's throat. I had blood all over my hands and my father kept on saying, "Hold the pan under the head," but the pig kept on moving, and I continued to close my eyes, even after the pig's entire head had been cut off. The pig continued to move, even with his head cut off. His eyes were still wide open and I couldn't look the poor pig in the eye.

"Good job, Pedrito," said my father, "you collected plenty of blood. Should make some good sausages. Mr. Shaffer loves them. We'll have to give him a couple."

"Doña María and her husband will also love some," added my mother.

"You won't catch me eating blood sausage," I thought to myself, but I didn't say it aloud. After the pig stopped moving, my father slit open his stomach and removed all the organs. "We use everything," he said, showing me the various parts of the body. "Some of these will go into the blood sausage. These intestines your mama will wash thoroughly, and we will stuff them with the meat and blood sausages. The liver and heart will make a great addition to the blood sausages."

"Don't forget the stomach," said my mother. "It will make some wonderful *menudo* stew."

"I don't think I want to eat some of those dishes," I told my parents. "They don't sound that delicious to me."

"One day you will learn to like them," said my father. "I too hated them when I was a kid, and then I developed a taste for all good things as I grew older."

"I'll take his word," I said to myself.

"Get me the sharp knife again, *mi corazón*," my father said to my mother. He never called her by her name but instead referred to her as *mi corazón, mi amorcito, mi querida,* or the like, and he always said it with such love and kindness. "And please get me plenty of hot water."

My father shaved the entire hog and then began to cut it into different parts—the front and back legs, the ribs. He washed and wrapped the head in a burlap sack, after seasoning it with dried peppers and salt and rubbing it entirely with garlic. He wet the sack thoroughly and placed it in a pit in the ground, covering it lightly with sand and then with hot coals. He threw some more wood on top and let it sit under the coals until the following morning.

"Tomorrow morning, Pedrito," he told me, "we will have the most wonderful barbecue from that head. A little salt and a little pepper, and some of your mother's great tortillas are all we need." He even promised to let me taste his favorite part, the brains. "No, *Papacito,* I don't want to eat the brains," I said. I don't know why, but I had just decided that at that age, I didn't want to eat brains. I didn't like the way they looked, that dirty white blob.

By the time my father had taken care of the head, my mother had washed and prepared all the innards. She refilled the pot with more water and when the water was boiling again, she threw the four big legs into it.

"We must boil these legs immediately, or they'll spoil, even in this cool weather," said my mother, explaining that the following day she would turn them into tamales and sausages, after curing the meat with plenty of peppers and some vinegar.

We only had one large pot, so when the legs were cooked, my mother removed them, threw out the water, and filled the pot with the outer layers of the pig. The fat melted, providing my mother enough lard to cook with for the rest of the winter. She would also use some to make soap. Swimming on top of the melted lard were those beautiful pieces of fried meat, *chicharrones,* which we would use the rest of the winter to season eggs, cook with rice, add to beans, and in many other ways. Unlike some other parts of the pig, I loved to eat them just the way they were, with a sprinkling of salt, particularly when they were still hot.

The rest of the meat was ground, with my parents taking turns at the ancient meat grinder mounted on an old tree trunk thicker than my entire body. It had been there since the days of *Tío* Jesús. I tried to help grind, but I didn't have that much strength. But my parents agreed I was very helpful, carrying the meats, keeping the cat away, and keeping little María Elena away from the fire.

"Bring me the vinegar," said my mother. She saturated the ground meat with plenty of it to help cure it and make it last longer. Then she poured into the mixture a large amount of ground red pepper that her mother had sent her from Mexico the week before. Lots of salt and lots of garlic followed. "A touch of herbs—some *comino* and some oregano—will finally do the trick," my mother said to no one in particular, as she seasoned. When the meat was well seasoned and well mixed, we began to stuff it into the innards my mother had washed and prepared. My job was to tie string to make the individual sausages, taking time to measure one of my outstretched hands between each knot. We hung the sausages out in the sun every day for seven days, making sure someone kept an eye on them so the buzzards and other animals would not steal them. We brought them in at night. After seven days, both my parents agreed the sausages were now dry enough to survive unspoiled for the rest of the winter.

By the end of the day, my parents were very tired, so they saved the cooked legs. The only thing left to do the following day was make the tamales.

On that Monday, which was still cool but not as cold as it had been on Sunday, my father removed the head that had been cooking since the day before and we had barbecue for breakfast. My mother also made me two sandwiches on tortillas, and although they were no longer warm at noontime, I still enjoyed the wonderful meat, which was so tender it fell apart. My father left for work; I left for school, and my mother went to work on the tamales.

When we returned home I could smell the tamales before I could even see our house. I immediately tasted one when I entered. "*Mamá*, I never watched before. How did you make those delicious tamales?" She agreed to give me a brief explanation. Elenita could have cared less.

"Well, first I grind the corn to make the *masa*. I mix the *masa* with some lard and red pepper flakes, salt, and black pepper. I cut the meat into little chunks and flavor it with spices, salt, pepper, chile powder, and a little garlic.

"Then I spread the *masa* lightly on the corn husks, like this," she said, picking up a tamale she made earlier. "I fill it with two teaspoons of meat, roll it up, and place it in the pot. Then I let them steam until the tamale stays firm and separates easily from the husk. And look at the results. Eight dozen beautiful tamales."

What a dinner we had that night. My mother made some of her wonderful Mexican rice and refried some beans to go with the tamales. I could have survived on nothing but tamales, but ate some of the rice and beans anyway. My mother took a dozen tamales to Mr. and Mrs. Shaffer, who always loved everything she cooked. She took another dozen to Juanito's parents, and she saved a dozen for Doña María, who would undoubtedly smell them all the way from her home and come around, as she usually did, holding her nose up and asking: "Do I smell something?" Sure enough, before we had finished dinner, she came by.

"What are you cooking, *mujer? Ay, qué huele bueno.* Those smells are making me hungry." She never really waited for answers or an explanation, but she would quickly pick up and devour a tamale, offering much praise to my mother for her wonderful cooking skills.

I never knew Doña María not to be hungry or begging for something to eat. She was never shy about it either. After she ate she would ask my mother: "And something to take to my dear old husband, God bless him?"

"But of course, Doña María," said my mother, giving her a small bag and sending her on her way. *"Gracias. Gracias. Qué Dios les bendiga."* She never stopped thanking my mother or tossing blessings upon all of us all the way to the farm's gate.

# Chapter 8

## "I Don't Mind Being Poor"

My mother always talked about how lucky we were and that we were so rich in so many ways, so I never considered myself poor. "That poor family at the end of the road, they are so poor. We must take them some tamales this afternoon," my mother said one day, blessing herself and thanking God because we were so rich by comparison.

"Part of the problem is that the father is so useless," said my father. "If he sees his kids are hungry, he should go catch some fish or shoot some rabbits. But he wouldn't know what to do with them."

"He hates to see animals die, his wife told me," my mother said.

As for us, we never went hungry. Somehow, my mother was able to cook a big meal every day, even if it was fish that my father and I had caught in the river, or a couple of rabbits my father had hunted down that afternoon. And of course, anytime we butchered a pig, there were plenty of tamales and sausages. Neighbors who loved my mother's tamales loaded us with *calabacitas* or tomatoes or eggs or whatever they grew in return. All the neighbors helped one another and no one starved or went hungry.

I suppose, when I think about it, that I knew Mr. and Mrs. Shaffer were rich because they had such a nice large home with inside toilets and electricity. But I never really thought about it, because my father and mother always said that one day we would also have a nice home with inside toilets and water and electricity.

"Sometimes you have to work many years to buy these things," my mother said. "Mrs. Shaffer's parents worked very hard in Germany and saved money to buy this farm. We will save some money and we will build our own home someday. And we will have all the things that rich people have."

One day I heard one of the kids in my class say to another as we rode on the bus home from school, "Pedro is very poor."

"Yes, I can tell by the clothes he wears," said another.

I was mad because somehow, the way they were whispering, it sounded like being poor was something very terrible.

"I heard you," I said. "How can you tell I'm poor? And why is it so bad being poor?" Despite instructions from the bus driver, who said we must never leave our seats when the bus was moving, I approached them as they sat two rows in front of me. The bus driver immediately shouted, "*Siéntate*, Pedrito." I returned to my seat, as one of the little girls volunteered, "Your lunch is always made of tortillas with eggs or beans. My mother goes to the store and buys the best white bread and expensive bologna for my lunch."

"Also," said the boy, "your shirts look like they're homemade. Ours come from the store. My mother goes to the stores in McAllen, usually Sears, to buy them. And you're darker than us. The poorer the people, the darker they are."

"That's because they spend so much time out in the sun, working in the fields," added the girl. "We don't have to work in the fields. My parents never had to work in the fields, like your parents."

"But I love tortillas better than white bread," I said, remembering that once Mr. Shaffer had given my father a loaf of white bread and nobody liked it. "And my shirts are always clean," I protested, and moved away to the back of the bus. I wish my friend Juanito was there that day, but he had stayed behind for religion classes and Sister would drive him home after school. I was very hurt, but I vowed I would not say a thing to my parents. I didn't want to hurt them, especially now that I had been labeled *poor*. It sounded like something inferior, unlike what my mother had always told me.

When I arrived home, my *mamacita* noticed there was something wrong. I wouldn't touch the apple she had left for my snack.

"*¿Qué pasa,* Pedrito?" she asked.

"*Nada, Mamá.*"

"*Sí,*" she insisted. "*Algo pasa.*" Something's wrong.

I told her some kids thought I was poor, and it sounded like something awful. I reminded her that she often spoke about us being so rich.

"We may be poor because we have no money, if lots of money is how they define rich. And we don't have a big house or a car or inside toilets," said my mother, as she sat me down next to her by the fire, where she was already preparing supper. "But we are so rich and so blessed in so many other ways. We never go hungry, for we have enough food and Mr. Shaffer is always sure that we have enough to eat. Your father works very hard and I work very hard, but we are blessed by the Lord with such good health," she continued. "Oh," she added, "We are also blessed with two beautiful children, and one day you and María Elena will become schoolteachers or doctors or something big."

She assured me that with all the money Elenita and I would make, after learning English and getting a great education, we would live very comfortably. We would be able to take care of her and my father in their old age. "Even if we have no money, we will still be rich. Who knows? We might even have grandchildren by then," she smiled and winked at me. "And, of course, Pedrito, we will always have one another. To me, that's rich."

She was smiling and crying at the same time. "Some people in San Antonio are poor and they have nothing to eat," she said, as she reminded me about the poor boys I encountered during our trip. "You can't grow vegetables on concrete in the city. You can't hunt for animals in the city, unless you want to eat rats and cats. I hear some of them have to, that's how poor they are," she said, which really scared me.

She had never said this before, but she continued: "Some of our relatives in Mexico are poorer than we are, Pedrito. Especially in areas where very few vegetables grow and where there is not much water. Not even rabbits survive in such hot climates. Going to bed hungry is the worst curse of the poor. We never do, so we are not poor."

*Mamacita* reminded me again of how lucky we were, repeating some of the things I already knew. We didn't have much money to buy food, only enough for the basics. But we had the hogs and the chickens we raised, as well as the vegetables, and the fish and rabbits my father and I caught. And when my mother helped Mrs. Shaffer can tomatoes, green beans, and corn, she always came home with her share of the canned goods.

My father milked Mr. Shaffer's cows every morning and always brought us some of the milk. My mother boiled it and when I came home from school, she always had a glass of milk for me. Sometimes, when my grandmother sent us Mexican chocolate, I would even have hot chocolate, particularly on cold winter days.

For special holidays, my mother would buy a can of Eagle milk, mix it with hot water, and melt a couple of squares of Mexican chocolate into it, and we had the most delicious and sweetest drink in creation. I was filled with joy whenever my grandmother in Mexico sent us chocolate tablets. She would always tell whoever delivered them that these were "for the children, my grandchildren."

We did have to buy coffee, rice and beans, salt and pepper, and white flour for tortillas. "But there is always enough money for these staples," my mother assured me.

"Mr. Shaffer does not make that much money off the farm, Pedrito," my mother said. "But he makes sure that we have enough, and he pays your father enough for us to buy these necessary items.

"He even told your father what a hard worker he is and that if someone offered him more money than Mr. Shaffer could afford, he would not stand in the way of us all moving to another farm to work. But your father likes it here and your granduncle Jesús spent all his adult life here too, working first for Mrs. Shaffer's parents. So until you children are grown, we will make our life in this little piece of land and this little house," she told me, as she rolled out the tortillas for dinner, and Elenita ran around singing.

"Don't forget, we have so much more than we would have if we had stayed in Mexico, *hijito.* Plus, you're learning English, you're getting an education, which your father and I never had."

When my father came home and learned what we were talking about, he joined the conversation as we all sat down to dinner. He told us, "Some families follow the crops all over the land, like some of our cousins, never spending more than a few weeks anywhere, never being able to send their children to school, never knowing if the next location will have enough crops to make them any money. They are always worrying how the bosses will treat them, and frequently they mistreat them. Sometimes they even whip the children who do not want to work."

"No, *Papá,* how horrible," I cried.

"So we'll just stay here until you children grow up," said my mother. "After that, maybe we will go back to Mexico, where you will teach English. Maybe when we're too old to work anymore," she said, looking very sad.

"Or maybe we'll move to the city, if we have enough money. Only God knows."

"No, *Mamá*," I told her, looking straight into her eyes. "When you get old, I will be old enough to work and I will support you and my father. Maybe you won't want to go back to Mexico. Maybe we can build a home of our own, like the parents of some of the children who go to school with me."

"Oh, Pedrito, you're such a dreamer! Never stop dreaming. Sometimes dreams do come true. But in the meantime, my son, just go to school every day. Go to school and learn every word and every sentence you can in English. That's how dreams come true. And ignore those kids in school."

After we had finished our rice and beans and tortillas, as she served my father and herself coffee, my mother thought of something. "You know what, Pedrito, tell those kids that no, you're not poor. Tell them you're a very rich and very lucky kid. And that you're rich because you can dream. Let them have some fun. Tell them you're wearing those clothes so people won't think you're rich and go after your money."

When I returned to school the next day, I sat at the back of the bus with Juanito. Because he lived in a house like ours and his parents worked like mine did, I guessed the kids who said I was poor would also consider him poor.

I pointed to a couple of kids sitting up front and told Juanito what they said. He told me to ignore them and sit with him from now on. Whether it was because they noticed that I had a bigger friend and they didn't want to mess around with him, or whether they felt badly about their remarks the day before, I don't know. But they didn't say anything to me and ignored me completely for several days.

About a week later, one of the kids, Leo, pulled me aside at lunchtime and asked if we could be friends. "Next time I have a party, Pedrito, will you come?" he asked me. He asked if I would exchange his white bread and bologna sandwich for one of my tortillas with eggs and beans.

"Sure," I said. I hated white bread, but my parents always taught me to be nice to the other children even if they weren't nice to me. But I couldn't refrain from teasing Leo: "Aren't you afraid someone might think you're poor and Mexican if you eat poor Mexican food? Or that you might become poor eating it?"

"You know, Pedrito, if eating Mexican will make me poor, I want to be poor like you."

"No, Leo, you don't want to be poor. Where did you learn about tortillas?"

"Oh, you see Nora up in front? Her mother makes them, and sometimes she shares one with me."

I promised I would bring him a tortilla the next day. "I wish my mother would make me tortillas and eggs or bean sandwiches for lunch, at least once in a while," he said. "You know, Pedrito, she doesn't know how. What's worse is I don't think she wants to learn. I hate that white bread and bologna. I'm so tired of it."

# Chapter 9

## My Friend Juanito

As the school days passed, I became closer friends with Juanito and frequently sat in the back of the bus with him and the older kids. When my mother allowed it, I went to play at his house, especially with his little lambs. Because he was older and taller, I looked up to him. He was always there to protect me when older kids teased me about being so short or laughed at the way I pronounced some words, although I didn't like to depend on him. We frequently met on the road to school and walked to the bus stop together. And in the afternoons we often walked home together, unless he had catechism classes. But as we approached the Christmas holidays, Juanito was missing from school. For three days, there was no Juanito in sight.

"Maybe he and his parents decided to go to Mexico early for the Christmas holidays," I thought. But Juanito liked school too much and I didn't think his parents would take him out of class. They would have waited instead until the holidays began. Also, who would take care of his little lambs? For sure, he would have asked me, I thought. After he had been missing for four days, I told my mother.

No, she said, she hadn't heard anything and Doña María had not come around with any news, either.

"I think Juanito must be sick or there is something wrong with his mother or father," I said.

"Don't worry, Pedrito. After dinner, I'll ask your father if we can walk over to see Juanito and his parents. It would be nice to wish them a happy and healthy Christmas."

When my father came home, he agreed we should all go see about Juanito. We were met at their door by Juanito's parents, Ramón and Alicia. They said Juanito had been very sick for several days.

"Doña María has been visiting him every day," said his mother. "She has made special teas and said all her prayers. We've all been praying. Nothing seems to work. He is burning. He's exhausted."

She started to cry, and her husband continued: "Juanito just lies there in bed. He has a very high fever. We wet his lips and keep a cool towel on his head. He's so weak, he sleeps most of the time."

We went inside and found Juanito in his bed. I touched him on the shoulder and said, "*Hola,* Juanito." He opened one eye slightly, but didn't smile and hardly seemed to recognized me.

"How long has he been sick?" asked my father.

"Remember last week, remember that very cold day *El Norte* arrived? He took the three little lambs over to the *arroyo,* and he fell in the water when one of the lambs pulled him. He came home shivering and wet all over. He caught a fever that night and has had it since," said Alicia.

My mother said, "Oh, when we brought you tamales, he seemed okay."

"I did see him in school last week," I said.

"Yes," said his mother, "he didn't want to miss, with the holidays coming up. I knew something was wrong, but he refused to say anything, until he could no longer continue, until his fever was so high you could feel the heat from across the room."

"It seems there is nothing Doña María can do and we don't know where to turn," Juanito's father said, as his mother sobbed softly.

"Have you tried *el Padrecito* Gustavo?" my father asked. "Besides being a priest, I understand he's also a doctor."

"I will go tomorrow to see if I can find him. He has such a huge territory to serve," said Ramón, "and now with Christmas, he must be very busy with all the extra services."

I looked out the back of their little house and noticed Juanito's lambs. He told me that his father butchered only two a year, one in the spring and one in the fall, so he always had six or seven with him. Last spring, two babies were born and his father sheared the heavy wool from the older ones, which his mother used to make a quilt for Juanito. I remembered how he loved his lambs and how he always regretted the day one was slaughtered. But, after all, like me with my little animals, Juanito also understood the lambs were there to provide the family with food. But when he and I walked the lambs to the water hole, Juanito said he only thought about the good times he had experienced while walking them to the *arroyo* to graze and to drink water.

It seemed like only yesterday that Juanito had asked me to come to his house after school and we could take his lambs to the *arroyo*. My parents approved, provided I didn't stay too long or asked Juanito's parents for any food. "Heaven knows, they don't have any more than we do, Pedrito!" said my mother.

I fell in love with Juanito's lambs and I asked my mother if after Juanito recovered, I could join him once in a while as he walked the lambs to the *arroyo*. "Of course, Pedrito, but not too often," she said, not wanting me to become a pest.

As Juanito lay sick in bed, I walked outside and although it was getting dark, I wanted to see the little lambs up close. "*Papá,* can we take them for a walk?"

"It's too late, Pedrito. One or two might run away, since they don't know us as well. Let's do it another day."

I agreed, but then Juanito's parents walked Elenita and me to the lambs and let us pet them for a few moments. They invited us to walk with them to the *arroyo* with the little lambs. It reminded me of the book we were reading in school about the three little lambs that were living up in the mountains somewhere far away where there was lots of snow. They belonged to a little girl and a little boy with very yellow hair.

There was nothing else we could do for Juanito, so after the short walk with the lambs, we returned home.

My mother said she still wanted to do a few things and make some preparations for Christmas. The next day was the last day of school, and in three more days, Christmas would arrive. My mother had lots of work ahead, especially making tamales, the traditional holiday food.

Trying to put on a happy face, on the way home from Juanito's I told my parents, "We had a visit from Santa Claus at our school this morning. Did you know about Santa when you were young?"

"Yes, Pedrito, in America he brings toys and gifts to children on Christmas Eve," said my mother. "In Mexico, we wait until January 6, the Feast of the Three Kings, to give the children their gifts."

"Tell me about the Three Kings," I said. I had heard about them, but I couldn't remember the details.

"They were the ones, Pedrito," said my father, "who followed a star and found the baby Jesus where he was born in poverty. They brought him many gifts. It's that tradition that we observe, as our children receive gifts from the Three Kings."

I told my parents that one kid on the bus home from school told me he was getting "many toys" from Santa. "That's because I'm a very good boy. Anyway," the boy told me, "Santa always gives more toys to richer kids, because rich parents give Santa lots of money."

I didn't tell that part to my parents.

"Pedrito, you and Elenita are getting something from Santa, too. And next month, we will celebrate the Feast of the Three Kings also. And if Juanito recovers by then, we will have him and his sister and their parents over for tamales."

My father added, "Everything here in America these days is Santa Claus. Santa Claus is coming to town. If we're going to be Americans, we might as well have Santa pay us a visit also. *¿Verdad?*"

"When are we becoming Americans, *Papá?*" I wanted to know.

"Oh, Pedrito, who knows? In many ways, we are American. And you were born in this country, so you already are an American." I was startled at the revelation. I had never considered myself anything but Mexican.

The day before Christmas, my father cut down a small mesquite tree and brought it home for us to decorate. We decorated it with ribbons my mother had around the house. We added a red paper bell and a yellow star Miss García taught us how to make out of construction paper in school the week before. We took pieces of cotton from an old pillow and wrapped them on the branches. "Ah, we have snow!" I thought. It wasn't quite as big, and it didn't look like the big, beautiful tree we had in our classroom. That one came from the north and Miss García said it was a "fir tree, a cold-weather tree." For this holiday, our hot-weather tree would work just as well. It was about my size and it sat perfectly on top of a bench in the corner of our little cabin.

On Christmas day, Elenita and I woke up early, and *Mamacita* and *Papacito* pointed to the tree, where Santa had left our gifts. We both ran and grabbed at packages as my mother explained which gifts were for whom. Elenita received a beautiful little doll and some socks. I got some socks and two pencils. We each received a coloring book and a box of crayons, just like the ones I had noticed at *La Marqueta* and had told my mother I wanted to have someday, when we had extra money.

"Thank you, Santa, wherever you are," I shouted out the door, hoping Santa was close enough to hear me, adding, "I hope you left something for Juanito also."

As I shouted, I noticed Doña María running toward our house.

"Maybe she wants to go with us to church," said my father. "Or maybe she wants to know if your *mamá* made some tamales for Christmas."

*"Dios mío, Dios mío, qué mal tiempo,"* she was crying.

*"¿Qué pasa,* Doña María?" my parents both asked at once.

*"El niño* Juanito, *se me murió.* He's dead. He died last night as the church bells rang to summon us all to Midnight Mass. I couldn't save him. I never had anyone die on me before. I think he died of pneumonia. He will be going straight to heaven, he was such a pure boy, a little angel." She continued talking nervously, without a break, as was her usual way. But this time she spoke more hurriedly than ever.

I had never known anyone who had died before, although I would hear from time to time that my granduncle, who had once lived in our house, had died and gone to heaven. I did know that everyone we knew who ever died went "straight to heaven, with God's blessings."

"Heaven is such a beautiful, peaceful place," my mother once told me when I asked about being dead, "nobody ever wants to come back."

"Have I lost my friend to heaven forever, *Papá?*" I asked.

"The Lord has called your friend to heaven," *Mamá* said as my father, who never seemed to cry, struggled to find the proper words.

"No, you have not lost him forever. Only in this world," he finally said.

"But I will never see Juanito at the bus stop or at school or with his lambs. Is that so?" I wanted to know. I couldn't stop crying.

"You will always have memories of him. And one day you will be together with him; we will all be together in heaven." They both embraced me and held me tighter than they'd held me in a long time. Everyone cried. It was comforting to see that even my father cried. Elenita was very confused by it, but she too cried.

I cried and cried and my mother said, *"Ya, niño, ya no llores,"* although she and my father couldn't stop either.

My father said, "Let him cry. It is good for him. It's good for all of us." He walked outside and I could see him walking behind our little house, just walking up and down slowly. I wanted to join him but my mother said, "He wants to be alone."

I couldn't understand why such a good boy had to die and why I had to lose this friend forever. If the good Lord wanted to take him, why didn't he wait until Juanito was an old man, which is when most people die? I would miss him so much in school, on the bus, and the few times we played together. He would no longer be there to walk with me home from school. I would have no one to protect me from the older boys. I hardly ever had any problems, but it was nice to know Juanito was around if I needed him. I knew his parents and his sister and his little lambs would miss him even more.

My father said he would go to see if Juanito's parents needed anything. When he came back, my father said he had helped Juanito's father make a box in which they placed Juanito. Later in the day, on a beautiful Christmas day, after we had gone to Mass, we went back to Juanito's house. My mother took some tamales, but Juanito's parents couldn't eat, for they were too upset. They both cried and hugged the box in which Juanito rested. Juanito's sister, Maruca, had gone to stay with Doña María because her parents did not want her to suffer the loss so heavily. She was too young to understand.

"My only son," cried his mother. "The Lord gave him to me on Christmas Eve, as the church bells were ringing for Midnight Mass. He took him back at exactly the same time, nine years later."

Ramón and my father picked up the box and carried it to the river. The rest of us, including six other neighbors, followed. My mother led us all in saying the Rosary as we walked slowly, with my father and Ramón carrying the box with Juanito's body. When we got to the river, Ramón and Alicia put the box in the river and, at the shallow point, simply pulled it across as they made their way to the other side. Another neighbor had crossed the river early that morning to give the bad news to the relatives, including the grieving grandparents. They were waiting across the river, all dressed in black, for Juanito and his family. They would bury Juanito in the little family ranch not far from the river.

We waved good-bye until they disappeared across the river. Then we walked silently back home. I cried every time I thought I would never see my friend in this life again.

# Chapter 10

## A Life on the Road

On a cold winter evening, my father's cousin Rubén, his wife Marta, who was also my mother's cousin, and their two boys, Roberto and Reynaldo, arrived at our home, hoping to spend the night before going on to Mexico the following day. I had never met any of them before and had so many cousins that unless I knew them in person, I got them all mixed up. So it was nice to meet these "new double cousins," as my mother explained, since they were related on both my father's and my mother's side of the family. Cousin Roberto was nine years old; his brother Reynaldo was seven. I was delighted to meet my two new *primos*.

"*Diosito mío, ¿de dónde vienen?*" my mother asked.

All of them were speaking at once, explaining that a trucker had just dropped them off at our gate and they had been riding "for hours, from very far," but I had no idea what that meant. "*Muy lejos,* very far," the kids said. Two days on the road, they said, but they weren't too sure where they were coming from. I never could catch the names of the cities or the states they were talking about, and when I asked again, my cousins would simply say, *"De otro pueblo, de otro estado. Muy lejos."* Yes, they were coming from another town, another state, very far away.

I did understand that the last couple of months they had been working on a farm two days away, where the man who drove them there and back had placed them. "He finds us the jobs and drops us off, and when the work is finished, he returns and picks us up," said Rubén. His wife added, "Sometimes he drops us off at another farm, but this time he said he had no immediate plans, so he brought us back here. It's been too long a time on the road."

"We have worked very hard, many hours. All four of us. It's been two very long years, my cousins," said Rubén. "Now, thanks to God and the Lady of Guadalupe, we can go home to see our parents, and the children can visit their grandparents. We want to spend a month or two, until it warms up," he said, explaining that the crops would not be ready for harvesting until March.

He continued, "We must never forget where we came from. Our children need to know their grandparents, and their grandparents should get to enjoy the children too."

Uncle Rubén explained that after visiting their relatives in Mexico, he expected the trucker to send word, perhaps stop by our home, to let them know when he would pick them up and take them to another job. Who knows where?

Luckily I didn't get the signal my mother and father usually gave me to go out and play when grown-ups were around, for I wanted to hear the entire story.

"It's very hard work, and the summers are brutally hot," added his wife, *Tía* Marta. "But what would we do in Mexico? Starve to death?"

They were all very hungry and my *mamacita* made them a big dinner of flour tortillas and eggs with tomatoes and peppers and some of her homemade sausages. And as usual, there were plenty of beans for all to enjoy.

"We never starve. We always have something to eat here," my mother told our cousins proudly, thanking God and Our Lady of Guadalupe and blessing herself, as she always did when she spoke about our good life. Marta blessed herself also, and my father and Rubén looked at one another, lowered their heads, and also blessed themselves.

"*Vamos a jugar,*" I invited my cousins, as I started out into the cool weather. I heard *Tía* Marta say, "My kids and your kids look so much alike. Let's hope they enjoy playing together and getting to know one another. It's good to know your blood relatives."

"Obviously, the same blood flows through all their bodies," said my mother. I wasn't too sure what that meant but ran out to play with my cousins, saying the words I had learned in school, "Let's go out and play." I soon realized they spoke very little English, and I was so proud to know that I spoke much more than they did.

"Do you like school?" Roberto wanted to know. "Yes," I said, and we went back into our house and I took out my notebook to show him and his brother what I was learning. They were both staring at my letters and numbers, which I had copied as carefully as I could from the ones written large on the blackboard by Miss García. "These words are *red, white,* and *blue,* the colors of the American flag, which has forty-eight stars, one for each state," I told them. "Miss García makes us copy all this from the board. She says it's important to learn to write clearly." I told them that Texas was one of the states represented by one of those stars and that maybe they had been to some states represented by other stars.

As we went through my notebook, their father, who was sitting nearby, explained, "There's been no time for school for my boys." He told me and my parents that when they were hired to work, the *may-*

*ordomo* made sure they understood there was no time for anything else.

"'You're being hired to work, not to play, not for the boys to go to school,'" Marta quoted him as saying, grateful that they did get a day off, Sunday, to rest, wash their clothes, shop, and do everything else.

"So, we've been picking cotton, harvesting crops, pulling up carrots, onions, zucchini, and green beans," explained my uncle.

His wife added, "The boys had to work alongside us, as difficult as it is for me to see it. They are still so young. But this is how we were contracted by the trucker, the *contratista.* We all have to work."

Aunt Marta explained that there had been an effort to teach the children. "Last summer, a teacher came by and tried to organize a class of the fifteen or so children between the ages of five and sixteen who lived in the camp where we were quartered. But he was only allowed to teach them on Sundays. Sometimes he tried after six o'clock in the evening, but it would soon get dark."

"*Ay,* there were so many obstacles," my uncle said, adding, "There was no light out in the fields, and no place big enough to hold the class. The teacher found it difficult to hold the attention of six-year-olds and keep order among the older children. After about a month of trying, he excused himself and we never saw him again."

"He really didn't want to go," continued my aunt. "The farmer told the teacher to get off his property." She said the teacher quoted the farmer as saying, "You're interfering with my work and my workers. I hire them to work, not to go to school. They can go to school on their own time, not mine."

"They're all the same, those farmers," said *Tía* Marta. "They want you to work from sunup to sundown. They're never satisfied."

"The farmer was mad," said *Tío* Rubén, "because the teacher told him that children, especially the very young, should not be working." The teacher had said children should be in school and that there's a law against six-year-olds having to work. But the farmer told the teacher that the laws only applied to American children. "If you're so worried about these children, take them back to Mexico," he told the teacher. "So," said Marta, "we had no choice, no school for our children."

"So you work. They feed you well, though. After all, they want you to be strong and healthy or you're no good to them," said Uncle Rubén.

"How far away did you go?" I asked my little cousins, as we walked away from the grown-ups and went to see our pigs.

"Very, very far. We drove for hours and hours."

"Farther than San Antonio?" I asked. I quickly added, "I went to San Antonio for my sixth birthday."

"Oh, much farther," they both answered.

"We passed San Antonio just a few hours ago. That's not far," said Roberto, the nine-year-old.

After we ran around and played and I showed them our pigs, goats, and *burro,* we settled down with our parents. We all sat on the ground outside and talked and visited until very late, drinking tea to keep warm. My father had not seen his cousin in a long time, so they had much catching up to do. And Marta and my mother said they had not seen one another since they were teenagers. Both Marta and Rubén had come from migrant families, going north to work on the crops for many years.

"Our parents did it before us. And our two boys will probably do the same when they grow up," said Marta. "What else is there to do?"

"Maybe one day they will go to school," said my mother.

"It's impossible!" said Marta. And my mother said no more.

"Maybe one of these days we will have enough money so we can leave them behind with my parents and they can go to school in Mexico for a year or two," said Marta. "Just to learn the basics. Just so they know how to sign their names."

"At least that," said my mother, "although it would be so much better if they learned a little English, like my Pedrito. He has learned so much English," she said proudly. She always wanted everyone to know about my English.

*Tío* Rubén and my father were engaged in their own conversation and it was difficult for me to follow both, since I was sitting closer to my mother. Elenita had fallen asleep on my mother's lap, and my mother said it was time to figure out how we would all sleep in our small room.

"*Mira, amor,*" said my father. "You and Marta and the children will fit in there," pointing to our little cabin. "Rubén and I will go and sleep on the bed of the truck. Just give us each a blanket."

The following morning, my parents and Rubén and Marta got up while it was still dark. My mother made coffee and tortillas so that everyone could have something to eat before departing. Before dawn, so as not to arouse too much attention from the Border Patrol, although they didn't bother you much if you were returning to Mexico, the four of them gathered their little bags and headed for the river, happy to be going home to see the rest of their relatives. The water would be cold, but they would be in it for only a few moments at the shallowest point.

"We'll return in a month, *primito,*" said Rubén. "The *contratista* said we might stay up the valley, picking oranges and grapefruits, for a couple of months. But nothing is ever definite. The *contratista* says the money is good. The money is always good, for him. He takes most of it, and we do all the work. After that, he said he would take us to New Mexico, where we had been before, maybe spend another year or so there. That's life and one must live it."

I secretly dreamed that I could go off to New Mexico with them. I even hoped that my cousins would stay with us so they could go to school with me. Perhaps I could also teach them everything I knew. But it was impossible. We didn't have room for them. Maybe their father could find a job with another farmer in our area, I dreamed.

"I think they enjoy being on the road," said my mother. "They don't see any other way, any way out of their cycle. And we must respect them for it."

Marta made her farewells and thank-yous as they left. "We'll see you again in a month or two. And maybe we'll see you again in a couple of years, if the *contratista* brings us back by here," she said.

"God willing, in a couple of years maybe we'll have an indoor kitchen and even running water," said my mother, as she took a handkerchief and wiped off Marta's tears.

"These are tears of joy, not of sadness," Marta assured my mother, as she kissed us all good-bye.

*"Primitos,"* I said to my cousins, "Next time you come we will go to the river and fish or maybe go hunting together." I was sad to see them go so soon.

# Chapter 11

## Off We Go Hunting and Fishing

"Pedrito, how is the homework situation?" my father asked one afternoon after he got home from work.

"It's finished," I assured him.

"*Bueno,* let's go fishing." And off we headed for the river, with our homemade fishing rods. We were able to fish more frequently in the late spring and summer, when the days were longer, but no matter when, I always enjoyed it. I enjoyed being with my father most of all, and we always seemed to have a good time when we went fishing or hunting.

We always managed to catch two or three fish for our dinner. If my father didn't recognize the fish, or if the fish was too small, he would throw it back into the river. Usually I watched my father fish, but this time, he decided to teach me a few lessons.

"This is the way to hold the fishing rod," he lectured. "Always tie the rope to the tree and sit on it."

"But why, *Papá?*"

"You're too small and too light and a big fish might pull you into the water." Despite his warnings, he sat nearby.

Suddenly there was a big pull on my line, and I screamed, "*Papá,* grab the line quickly." I was glad that the rope was tied to the tree behind us. At the end of the line was a large turtle, almost as heavy as me. I couldn't even pick it up.

My father was very strong, from all the hard work he did, but I could see sweat on his dark face, the muscles on his short legs bulging as he pulled.

"No need to fish for more," my father said. "Let's take this home to your mother, who will make us some great soup."

*Mamacita* made the best turtle soup I had ever eaten. Come to think of it, I don't remember ever eating anyone else's turtle soup. I watched with fascination as she prepared the soup in the big pot on the fire outdoors. She would chop onions and peppers and garlic and other spices and toss them into the boiling water with the turtle meat. Near the end, she even tossed in turtle eggs that had not yet hatched. When she served the soup, she placed an egg in each bowl. I didn't feel like eating mine, simply explaining that I liked eggs for breakfast but not in soups. Especially turtle eggs.

"*Ay*, Pedrito, how silly you can be," my father said, but he didn't force me to eat the egg. Instead, he reached in my bowl and put the egg in his mouth, as Elenita laughed. There was so much soup that my father and I took some to our neighbors Ramón and Alicia, Juanito's parents. And as always, there was some for Doña María and her ailing husband.

On one of our hunting trips, my father said, "Pedrito, you're still too young to hold a rifle. But always watch what I do, so when you grow older, you'll know exactly what to do." He talked to me about the importance of never pointing the weapon at a person. "Never! And before you shoot, you must make sure you're aiming at a javelina or a rabbit. Never aim at a deer, except in December or early January, during hunting season, or we will all go to jail." And he always warned me about carelessness. "You must always make sure there's not a person in sight. Too many accidents. Too many people have been killed or injured because of carelessness." As far back as I can remember, he was always warning me about something.

"I'm afraid of rifles, *Papá*. I don't know if I'll ever shoot one," I said.

"Some people abuse them and shouldn't have them. We need them for survival, Pedrito. As you can see, a couple of rabbits means we can have a nice stew with meat for our dinner. Or if your mother prefers, a nice meal of barbecued rabbit. Or how about rabbit and rice, *hijito?* Mmmm."

I remember the day *Papá* killed a javelina. "Javelinas are cleaner than pigs," my father said, adding, "Pigs eat anything, mostly leftovers. Javelinas are very selective. They look for the best herbs they can find, and the nicest vegetables and corn they can steal from the farms. But they have less fat than pigs, and therefore the meat is a little tougher and your *mamá* must cook it longer."

"*Ay, Papá,* our pigs eat anything and everything!" I said. "Like all our leftovers. Sometimes I want to throw up."

"But you know, Pedrito, I always like to give them some corn, or some of the milk from our goats. Corn and milk make for a better-tasting pig," he explained as we dragged the javelina home.

"Just wait and see what wonderful tamales your *mamá* will make for us with this baby. She'll need to add a little lard from the last pig, though." he added.

She sure did, and I couldn't tell the difference from the pork tamales. Maybe it had to do with the peppers and the garlic and the other spices. Anyway, they tasted good. *Mamá's* tamales always tasted good, and I always told her so. I had to make up for the times I couldn't eat some of her food.

I knew that the blood sausage smelled terrific, but I couldn't get myself to eat it. The *menudo* she sometimes made with the cow's or goat's innards and stomach also smelled delicious, but I just couldn't eat it either. My portion usually went to Mr. Shaffer or Doña María. We always had tortillas and beans, so when I didn't like the main dish, I simply made a taco filled with beans.

"One of these days you will eat all these," *Papá* said, adding, "and you'll regret not having tasted them in your early years."

"Maybe someday, but not today," I would answer every time the issue came up.

Whenever we went fishing or hunting, I liked to sing the songs and recite the poems I was learning in school.

*Jack and Jill went up the hill*
*To fetch a pail of water . . .*

Funny, we usually went down the hill, not that it was much of a hill, to the river to get a pail of water. Sometimes my father would tell me to stop singing.

*"No, hijito,"* my father would say. "You can sing when we fish because the fish don't mind. But don't make any noise when we get to the field. We don't want to scare the rabbits or the javelinas away. After we take our game, you can sing as much as you like all the way home."

One day we were out only a few minutes when my father shot two nice, fat rabbits. I always shut my eyes and covered my ears, but my father would again lecture me about the need to hunt for our survival. When we had our meals, my father and my mother always thanked the Lord for providing the food, and they also prayed for the animals. "May they multiply, dear Lord," my father said, to which my mother added, "So the poor may have more food."

After we had our two rabbits, we were ready to go home and my father said, *"Ahora,* Pedrito, go ahead and sing. Maybe I can learn to sing some of your American songs too."

*Mary had a little lamb, little lamb, little lamb . . .*

The song brought back thoughts about my friend Juanito, who had died tending to his little lamb. I couldn't continue.

*"Qué pasa, hijo,"* said my father.

*"Nada,"* I said.

Suddenly a large rattlesnake jumped from the brush a few feet in front of us. My father dropped the rabbits, reached for his gun, and shot the rattlesnake in the head.

When it stopped moving, my father poked it with a long stick to make sure it was dead. Then he took the rope he always carried and tied it around the snake's neck, and we carried it home. The snake was taller than my father. "It's about seven feet long," he said. "The skin is beautiful. I will take it off and sell it. Some people eat rattlesnake meat, but we don't. Mostly *Americanos,*" he said.

As far back as I can remember, my parents had warned me about rattlesnakes, for there were so many in our area. When my father and I slept outdoors because of the heat, we would put a rope around our bedding to keep the rattlesnakes out. "They normally don't attack you unless you move or tease them. But they are deadly. Very poisonous. So many people have died of snakebites," he said.

"Do you know any?" I wanted to know.

"I don't think I ever told you about your great-grandmother Fela and her encounter with a rattlesnake, back around 1865," my father said.

"Tell me, tell me, *Papá,*" I said. I had heard him mention it before but had never heard the full story.

"I will tell you," he said, as we walked home slowly, me carrying the rabbits and he dragging the rattlesnake.

"My great-grandparents, Gabriel and Fela, developed a small piece of land about five miles south of the Rio Grande, the same farm where my father and his father were born. It was difficult, and practically nothing but cactus and mesquite grew there, but somehow, they survived and so did—barely—their children, and their children's children and their great-grandchildren. At the time of my great-grandparents, the nearest farm was four hours away by horse. But the young couple was desperate to make a life of their own and picked land no one else wanted. Soldiers of fortune, adventurers, and government troops sometimes came through, sometimes stealing what little Gabriel and Fela had. But they held on, fiercely independent and wanting to make it on their own.

"When soldiers came by the farm, Gabriel and Fela made sure not to take sides on the political situation, saying they knew nothing. They welcomed all the strangers, taking care not annoy any of them. When they asked questions, my great-grandparents would humor them. 'Did the *Federales* (meaning the federal troops) pass by here recently?' bandits wanted to know. 'Yes, two or three days ago, they were headed south,' Gabriel would say. 'Did you see a group of about a dozen bandits on horseback pass by?' the *Federales* wanted to know. '*Sí, mi capitán,* they were headed for the river,' Gabriel would inform them. Fela usually served the men tortillas with beans and let them fill up their water canteens, and the men went happily on their way, seeking the enemy. But Gabriel knew neither side could be trusted and had heard that entire families had been massacred by the revolutionaries or the soldiers.

"Twice a year, Gabriel went to Monterrey for supplies, and he often stopped halfway there to visit his parents. Sometimes he took his wife and left her with his parents while he continued on to Monterrey. But one day she insisted that she would be fine staying by herself. Besides, now that she had a four-year-old daughter and a two-year-old son, traveling was much more difficult. 'If any *bandidos* or *Federales* go by, I'll make them some tortillas and give them water. They won't hurt a woman alone with two children,' she assured her husband.

"The day after Gabriel left, Fela was in the field hanging some clothes out to dry. She shook out a piece of clothing before hanging it and the noise must have attracted a rattlesnake that thought it was being attacked. She felt a sudden sting behind her knee and looked back to see a large rattlesnake slithering away.

"What to do? She knew that in those days the only remedy for such a bite was to take a knife, cut a cross through the bite, and suck out the poison. The wound was in such a position, though, that she could not reach it. With two kids, she could not walk to the nearest farm, for she felt that the poison would spread and there was not much time left.

"So she prayed that her husband would return sooner than expected. She even hoped some stranger would come by, something she always feared. In the meantime, she went to work making lots of tortillas, boiling water for the children to drink, cleaning the little house, and washing all the clothes. It was very hot and very humid, but she kept working and sweating and getting weaker and more tired by the minute as she continued to work. She told her four-year-old daughter that *Mamá* might go on a long, deep sleep, and if that happened, to make sure she drank lots of water, gave her little brother water too, and ate tortillas until their father returned.

"She prayed and prayed for the return of her husband and couldn't sleep all night long. She was worried about dying, but much more about the survival of her children without her. She finally fell asleep at dawn, but woke up when the baby was crying and the sun was shining through their little window. The high fever she had after the bite was gone, and she was very much alive and feeling much better and quite rested.

"'It's miraculous,' she thought, 'the good Lord and the Blessed Virgin of Guadalupe have kept me alive.' Usually the fever only intensifies after a snakebite and keeps on getting worse until you die. But she survived.

"Some family members believed that the worry, the heat, the work she did to prepare for her death, and her fear for the survival of her children made her sweat so much that she sweated out the poison. But others argued that perhaps the snake was not poisonous. The more religious relatives to this day always say it was a miracle from God and Our Lady of Guadalupe. Anyway, it remains one of the happiest stories of survival in our family history."

"Looks like you've been telling another family story," my mother said to my father on our arrival, for he was still talking when we arrived home, and she was waiting patiently for him to finish.

"*Sí, querida,*" he smiled and winked.

"*Ay, ¿qué es eso?*" my mother asked, almost shouting. Of course she knew it was a snake, and she said she didn't want any part of it. My father explained that he would sell the skin, as usual, and toss the meat to the pigs.

"You just go ahead and do that," she said, as she took the rabbits, hung them on a pole, and skinned them while the fire roared. After she rubbed spices all over them, she put them on the grill, and we sat around waiting for another great meal.

# Chapter 12

## "Tell Me Another Family Tale"

Every evening, my mother would cook supper outdoors, and after dinner, we would stay there, sitting on the ground, talking, laughing, telling stories, and practicing our English. We were always disappointed when it rained or when it was too cold to remain outdoors, but as we headed toward spring, we could spend more time in the fresh air.

We usually followed the same ritual: My mother would wash the dishes. My father would offer to help. *"No, mi amor,"* my mother would tell him, "you work too hard all day. So sit down and relax. Practice your English with the children. I will listen." My mother was less willing to try the lessons, especially at the beginning. "I can't say it," she would complain. But she always managed after we kept prompting her.

So my father would sit with Elenita and me, and if the days were getting shorter and the nighttime coming earlier in the winter, we would light a lamp while we waited for our mother to join us. We had half a dozen rugs that my mother had made from the sheep and the little lambs we had slaughtered, and we placed them on the ground to keep us warm. Sitting on those rugs brought back memories of the little lambs I had grown to love over the years, only to see them slaughtered. But as my mother would say, "Such is life. And you have those beautiful rugs to remind you of them."

Yes, I remembered them well. I could even remember their names. I always liked to sit on the skin of a lamb I called Chico. And the one my sister liked was once a goat named Tata. She had brown spots and made for a very beautiful little rug.

The lamb rugs also reminded me of my friend Juanito. "Is Juanito in heaven?" I asked. *"Sí, niño!"* both my parents replied at once. They never wanted to spend too much time talking about Juanito.

For our nightly rituals, my father would sit on one side, facing the lamp; my mother, when she eventually joined us, sat on the other side. Elenita would hardly sit for long. Instead she would usually run around the circle, play some of her imaginary games and talk to her imaginary friends, and sing nonsensical songs as if no one else was around. I think she had no idea what some of the words she used in her songs meant. Some of them weren't even words. Not that I knew, anyway. Eventually, she would end up on my father's or mother's lap, usually falling asleep long before we were ready to retire for the evening. I would lie on the leftover lap and sometimes also fall asleep while my parents were still talking.

But I would stay awake if my father was telling a good family story.

One cool evening, my father did not light the lamp. My mother asked: *"Qué pasa,* José? It's getting dark. You're not lighting the lamp?"

"No, Guadalupe, Mr. Shaffer told me to make sure not to light up anything outdoors tonight."

*"Por qué, querido?"*

"Well, America has declared war against the Germans, who want to come over and take over the entire world, according to Mr.

Shaffer. President Roosevelt and his generals believe there are German planes flying near the Rio Grande, looking for targets and for places where they can land safely and invade our country. Or at least spy on us, since there are no soldiers around here to fight back and the population is so sparse. They may even be scouting around to establish a fort here."

"*Diosito,* keep them away from us," my mother said, looking up toward heaven and crossing herself with her rosary. *Mamacita* brought her rosary with her every night when we sat outside and silently recited it while we spoke and ate. She could pray and talk at the same time, even when I urged her to listen to my English lessons, worried she would not learn anything.

"What is going on, *Papito?*" I wanted to know.

"As you know from what Miss García has been telling you, our country is at war, *hijito.*"

"I know, but why do people want to fight? I thought only roosters and bad kids in school fought."

"No, *hijo.* As I told you the day we went to listen to Joe Louis fight, some people want to fight us for real. They want to take over this country. But President Roosevelt and his generals will not let them. Unfortunately, Mr. Shaffer told me today his son Jerry will be going into the army to help us fight the enemy. In the meantime, we must do our part, like not lighting the lamp outside so that the German planes will not see us."

"I'm afraid of war, *Papito.*"

"Don't worry, *niño,* we're going to be OK."

Little by little, I learned more about Germany, a far-off land where Mr. Shaffer's parents had come from. I couldn't understand why Mr. Shaffer was so nice and other Germans were at war with us. I was too afraid to talk about the war. I looked at the sky, sitting on my skins, and noticed the beautiful, big moon and thousands of stars.

"How far away are the moon and the stars, *Papá?*"

"Very, very far," said my father.

"Miles and miles away," said my mother, who still seemed worried about the Germans and was praying even more intensely and louder. "*Diosito mio y la Virgen de Guadalupe,* keep those Germans away."

"Are the moon and the stars as far away as San Antonio?" I was eager to know.

"No, *hijito,*" my father said. "Much farther."

"Are they as far as where the waters of the Rio Grande begin to flow?"

"No, *hijito.* Much farther."

"They don't seem to be that far. I'll have to ask Miss García," I said. "Maybe she knows."

My parents seemed embarrassed and I felt bad for asking, but my father changed the subject: "It's time for our lesson, Pedrito. Tell us what you learned in school today."

"Yes," said Elenita. "Let's do the ABCs."

So for the next few minutes, we recited the ABCs and then sang them, one at a time, as far as I could go, which was LMNOP. Elenita always wanted to be first, although she frequently mixed up some of the letters and I had to correct her.

"No, Elenita, it's DEFG, not DFGB."

"*Déjala,* leave her alone," *Mamita* said. "She's still young. She'll learn. Let me try it: ABCDEFG HIJKLMNOP." That's the best my mother had ever done and she looked very proud.

"*Perfecto,*" said my father, and we all applauded. My mother confessed that she had been practicing in the daytime, as she went around doing her chores.

We continued doing the letters up to P, and the numbers up to ten, and singing "Mary Had a Little Lamb" until Elenita fell asleep in the arms of my father.

But my mother and father and I continued until I was tired of repeating the same thing over and over. Sensing my reluctance to continue, my father asked, "What else are you learning in school, my son?"

"We are still working on 'I pledge allegiance to the flag' and we are also learning to sing something called 'My Country 'tis of Thee,' but I still don't know all the words, *Papá*." I promised to share these with him later in the year. The night was still young, so I asked my father to tell me another of those family stories that had been passed down from generation to generation.

"Tell me the one about Great-grandfather Gabriel and his trip to Laredo, the one you promised to tell me the other day," I begged.

"All right," said my father. "Remember Gabriel was the husband of Fela, the lady who survived the snakebite?"

"Yes, I remember," I said.

"Remember he went shopping in Monterrey the time the snake bit her? Well, two years later he went on a trip across the river to Laredo," said my father as he told that story.

"Laredo was a hundred miles upriver. Gabriel estimated it would take him two days to ride there and two days to return, plus a day for shopping. Cloth and other goods came from across the big seas up the Rio Grande by boat and could only be obtained in Laredo, so he went there, on horseback, to buy several items for his family and one of his friends who lived a day away from their farm. The whole trip would take five days.

"On the fifth day, Gabriel failed to return. And the sixth and seventh and eighth day passed, and still no Gabriel. Day after day, Fela would await his return, sitting by the front door. She would not cry in front of the children, but when they were in bed, she stayed awake crying most of the night.

"In her mind, she knew nothing was wrong. 'Who knows, maybe the boat with the goods has not arrived or ran into storms across the seas,' she thought one moment. And at another moment, 'Maybe Gabriel met some friends along the way and decided to stay and visit for a couple of days. But Gabriel wouldn't do that. It's not like him,' she corrected herself.

"Each night she would put her children to sleep. The two-year-old boy did not understand, but the six-year-old daughter missed her father so her mother explained, 'Go to sleep, my daughter, for tomorrow your father will probably return from Laredo.' Then Fela would cry until, exhausted, she would finally fall asleep.

"After three weeks, when a cousin stopped by on his way from the north, she asked him to notify her parents, who lived on a farm on the road to Monterrey, that Gabriel had been gone for much longer than expected. Her parents arrived two days later. What could have happened, they wondered. They feared the worst.

"And to Fela's dismay, they weren't shy about expressing the worst: 'Poor Gabriel,' said her mother, 'he probably drowned.' 'Maybe he was killed by the *bandidos,* or the Indians,' said her father. He knew Gabriel was a peaceful man and would never fight, 'but you never know when you run into bad people,' he argued.

"'No, *Papá,* don't say that,' Fela begged.

"But Fela's parents agreed that she and her children could not remain on the farm by themselves. They must return with her parents to their home where she would raise her children as best she could. 'We'll find a way, but you can't stay here by yourself,' said her mother, mindful of the fact that there was already a food shortage and they didn't need the extra three people.

Fela was in no hurry to leave. As they prepared the children for departure and said some prayers, Fela prayed to the Archangel Gabriel and Our Lady of Guadalupe for a miracle. She reminded them of the miracle when she was bitten by the snake two years before. 'The horse isn't back. If Gabriel had drowned, the horse would have found his way home,' Fela told her parents, still not willing to accept the possibility of her husband's death.

"'True, *hija*,' said her father, convinced something was very wrong. 'Maybe the horse also drowned. Or maybe the soldiers or *bandidos* killed or stole the horse.'

"'My parents are not being very sympathetic,' thought Fela, who refused to give up hope.

"Nevertheless, they continued to prepare for that inevitable move south with her parents. Suddenly they heard a horse and a rider. It was Gabriel! After being greeted with lots of tears, lots of laughter, and lots of food, he explained that there had been a great flood in the river and there was nowhere and no way he could cross. He had to camp out for days and was eventually invited to a nearby farm to spend the rest of the time. As soon as the flood receded and the currents calmed down, he made his way home."

It seemed that every time Gabriel went away, something terrible happened. He vowed never to leave home again. Of course, it was a promise he couldn't keep. But there were no other stories to tell about them, at least not this interesting, said my father. "And if there were, no one bothered to pass them down to my generation."

I could hardly wait for my father to finish his story. As soon as he did, I fell asleep. As usual, he picked me up and took me into our little house, while my mother carried Elenita, and they placed us side by side on the floor on a quilt, with the rugs all around us, a ritual repeated almost every night of our early childhood.

# Chapter 13

## A Matter of Privacy

Our outhouse was about forty feet from our house, according to my count, and thirty feet according to my father's count. When I asked my mother, she said, "I never counted. Don't get me involved."

Sometimes I sat in that outhouse longer than I could stand the smell, but it was one of the few places where I had any privacy, and even a six-year-old sometimes wants to be alone. When I stayed there too long, usually reading one of my books, my mother would shout, "Pedrito, are you all right? Are you sick?" If I didn't respond immediately, she would wait a few minutes and then ask, "Did you fall down the hole, *niño?*"

Living in a small one-room house, there was little space to move around and get away from everyone else, especially when all four of us were inside during very cold days. We spent much of our time outdoors, but even there I could never sit alone. Elenita would be running around me, wanting to play or to recite the alphabet. Or she would be asking me silly questions.

"*Mamá,* please tell Elenita to leave me alone. I have to read my book for school."

It was no use. Elenita would disappear for a few minutes and then return, asking me to read to her from my book. And usually, both Elenita and my mother were within breathing distance.

I dreamed of being older so I could go to the river with the older boys, or go hunting by myself, or just take a walk in the woods. *Solo.* All by myself. No one else! But my parents feared for my safety and wouldn't let me go anywhere unless an older person was around to look after me. There weren't too many older people around and available to take me places. But even if there were, I didn't want anyone around at certain times.

"You must never go anywhere alone, Pedrito. It's very dangerous," my mother told me many times. But although I sometimes feared being outside in the dark, I really wasn't that scared in the daytime and I didn't see why I was so protected. I thought I was old enough to walk to and from *la marqueta* to take the school bus by myself, especially now that Juanito, who used to walk me all the way home, was dead.

I remember Juanito once told me how he also liked to be alone once in a while, even though he too loved his parents and his sister. He always felt so free when he walked alone to the *arroyo* with his little lambs. "Sure, the lambs are there, but I don't have to talk to anyone and no one has to talk back to me," he said. After Juanito was gone, my mother and Elenita met me at *la marqueta* after school every day. Before he died, he had been attending catechism classes in the church near our school, twice a week, to prepare for his First Communion. On those days, my mother picked me up at *la marqueta.* Juanito was driven home, along with several other kids from the ranches, by the two nuns who taught in the Catholic school and also taught catechism. The next year, I would probably be going to catechism classes also, and maybe have a little more freedom and some time to myself. I loved my parents and deep inside I understood their concerns. But even at my young age, I thought they were being overprotective.

I dreamed that one day I would have the freedom to walk to *La Marqueta* by myself, buy a penny lollipop, and sit there and listen to the radio for an hour, without having to think about chores around the house or the farm. It was only about a ten-minute walk, even if the walk was over a deserted country road.

One day I decided to take a walk down to the river. Alone. Without telling anyone. My mother was weeding vegetables behind the house, just before she would start cooking dinner. I had just arrived from school. Elenita was by my mother's side and my father was still at work.

"No one will know I'm gone," I thought. "I will only be gone for a few minutes. Everyone is too busy."

I enjoyed the walk. I cut a twig from a short tree and swung it like a bat as I walked and sang the latest song I had learned, "Old McDonald Had a Farm," except that I would change it to "Old Mr. Shaffer Had a Farm." What a luxury, being alone. I vowed I would not go near the water, for my parents would be too upset. "But they can't be too upset with me taking this short walk," I thought. "I'm not doing anything wrong. Anyway, they haven't warned me about going anywhere by myself in the last few days, so maybe they don't care as much anymore."

But they did care. Shortly after I left, as I later learned, my mother returned to the house and noticed I was gone. She started to shout for me, running around to see if I was by the animals or behind the house in the vegetable garden. But I was too far away and couldn't hear her calling. She ran to Mr. Shaffer's field, with Elenita running behind her. My father heard her screaming and started to run toward her, screaming back, *"¿Qué pasa, mujer, qué pasa?"*

*"Ay, Dios mio, ¿dónde está* Pedrito? *"* my mother was crying, trying

to explain that I had disappeared and that she feared I might drown or get lost in the woods. My father told her to control herself, that he would go looking for me. They doubted I would have gone to Juanito's, since Juanito had died, although they thought there was a possibility I might have gone to visit his lambs.

My mother went to Juanito's home anyway, just in case, and to ask Juanito's mother to join her in searching the woods for me. Juanito's father was away at work. My father headed for the river, and I was already on my way back when we ran into each other. I could tell by his facial expression and the tone of his voice that he was very mad, but I said, *"Hola, Papito. ¿Qué pasa?"*

*"¿Qué pasa?"* he repeated. "That you've scared the day and night out of everyone. Your mother is very upset! She thinks you may have drowned. You know how afraid she is of people drowning."

"Where is my mother?"

"Your mother and Juanito's mother and sister and Elenita are out looking for you in the woods. We must find them soon, before your mother dies of worry. You've been told many times never to go anywhere by yourself."

"But I thought that was when I was much younger, *Papá*. I'm six and a half now, going on seven."

"Your mother and I have never punished you before because you've been a very good boy, Pedrito. But this time we will think of something."

"What will you do to me, *Papá?*"

"Maybe we'll tie you to a tree and let you rot there." I couldn't imagine my parents would be so cruel, but I started to cry anyway. "Who knows?" My father continued, "we'll probably even take you out of school. If you're going to rot anyway, what's the sense of you wasting time going to school?"

I cried all the way home, and we continued toward the woods to the north of our house to look for my mother and Elenita and Juanito's mother and sister. I was still crying when we ran into them, and my mother promised, as she twisted my ears, "Save those tears for when I really punish you. You'll need them then."

I couldn't eat when dinnertime came along. My father and mother talked to me about the importance of obeying rules, and they made me promise never to walk away from the farm unless they knew where I was going and with whom.

"As you grow older, Pedrito, we'll be giving you more freedom to roam around," said my father. They spoke to me about a kid who disappeared some years ago on the way to *la marqueta* and was never seen again. "They think someone picked him up and took him up north to work on a farm, like a slave," said my mother. "Or maybe he went to San Antonio to join the other orphans on the street," said my father, putting fear in me. I had never heard that story before and wondered if they were making it up, although we never lied to anyone in our family. That evening, no one had time nor desire for lessons.

My father said he needed a shave. He took the knife and the strop on which he sharpened it, along with a pot of warm water and some soap, to his usual place by a mesquite tree. His father gave them to him on his seventeenth birthday, he told me. I enjoyed watching him shave, but this time I sat farther away than usual. No one was saying anything. Certainly no one was in the mood for singing. My mother did go on with her Rosary, thanking Our Lady of Guadalupe for bringing me back home safely.

Lucky for me, my father never tied me to the tree, and my mother never spanked me, which I thought she would do. For many days I wondered when that punishment would come. The biggest punishment was that the punishment never came. Apparently, they decided against it or they forgot the whole thing. Soon we were back to our lessons and discussions of what I had learned in school that day, or what the next page in my book was all about. And they wanted to know if I had learned the words of the latest song so we could all sing together.

But none of this made it any easier for me, and I still felt desperately that I needed some time to myself. I realized no one else was going to make such time for me, so I had to find ways to provide it myself. I offered to go into our garden to water the plants, just by myself. "No, *Mamita,* let me do it. I'm a big boy now," I said. It wasn't so much that I wanted to water the plants but that I wanted to be alone. It was only a few feet from the house, but I was alone. When I didn't have school, I enjoyed walking slowly into the fields to bring lunch and water to my father, just to savor that moment alone. Sometimes I would simply sit near him, neither of us saying a word.

"Sometimes, I need to be alone," I told my mother.

"Why in the world would you want to be alone, *niño?*" my mother answered. I didn't even try to explain.

I was still sitting in that outhouse from time to time too. I had heard that water toilets they build inside the home do not stink, but I also heard one of our neighbors tell my parents one day that they used to live in a house with an indoor toilet and that the whole house stank as a result.

"There is nothing like an outhouse," he said. "Much more comfortable, and away from everyone." His wife didn't agree. "I'd rather put up with a little stink than go lift up my dress in an outhouse on a cold winter night," she said, laughing and making my father blush and making my mother say to me and Elenita, "Run and play and sing your new song, children."

I couldn't imagine having the toilet inside the house or near the kitchen. The first time I saw an inside toilet was when I went to San

Antonio with my father. I did visit one in school almost every day. But I never sat on one of those stools, no matter how much I had to go. Some of the children complained that water splashed on their naked behind. One day, the water came up high when my friend Roel was still sitting and he got all wet when the water overflowed. The janitor found him crying and his pants were all wet. The janitor called the principal, who drove Roel home because he was too wet and too upset to return to class. Word got around fast and it was many days before other kids stopped kidding Roel about it. He hated going to school because of the teasing. As for me, I wasn't ready to take a chance. I was happy going to my outhouse.

# Chapter 14

## *Cascarones y Palmas*

One day, after driving Mr. Shaffer to the valley for business, my father returned with a truck full of palm fronds.

"*¿Qué es eso, hombre?*" my mother asked my father.

"Can't you see, they are palms, *mujer, palmas.*" Of course my mother knew, but when she didn't know something ahead of time, she always asked. What she really meant was, "What are those for?"

My father explained that one of the farmers up the valley had cut more than he could sell to be used for Palm Sunday. It appeared the palms were going to be thrown away. "As I drove by with Mr. Shaffer, I had an idea," my father said. He asked Mr. Shaffer if he could drop him off at the First State Bank so that he could seek out the farmer with the palms. Mr. Shaffer, who usually spent at least an hour at the bank while my father waited, agreed. Sure enough, the farmer was happy to get rid of the palms. "You're doing me a favor," the farmer told him. "He was grateful," said my father, "for he would have had to pay to get the palms off his property." Soon, my father had a truck full of palms.

Before the week was out, *Papá* had used the palms to attach a roof, about the size of our cabin, across the front of the cabin. "What did we ever do without it?" my mother wondered later.

It helped keep our little house cooler, and my mother could do many of her tasks in the shade. And Elenita and I had a place to play in the shade. Or I could sit there and read. When my father was building the roof, my mother handed him the palm we had received in church on Palm Sunday.

"Put it there with the others," my mother said. "It's blessed. It'll bless our new roof and our entire house." I could hear my father's annoyance and growl, but he obeyed. "God forbid lightning should strike us," he said.

The roof went up just in time for Easter.

We had been anticipating Easter in school for several weeks, since it meant a three-day holiday.

About a month before, Miss García asked all the children to collect eggshells so we could make *cascarones* and have an Easter party. My mother saved eggshells every day, careful to break them at one end to save as much of the shell as possible. In school, Miss García taught us how to cut construction paper into tiny little squares, which we would use to fill up the shells. Then we covered the top of the shells with onionskin paper, pasting it on with glue we made with flour and water.

"We have enough eggs to start decorating," Miss García said one day. "Each of you gets ten eggs, and I want to see some beautifully painted eggs when you finish." She drew some large eggs on the board and colored them with multicolored chalk to give us ideas, but she indicated that we should let our imaginations go wild.

"The brightest, most original *cascarón* will win a prize. And if we make many bright and beautiful *cascarones,* I will bring in extra prizes," she said. I knew my artistic talents were not equal to some of the other kids in our class and never expected to win a top prize. But I had fun decorating my *cascarones.* I used every color in my box to paint funny-faced characters, including a cat and a dog. "Is that really a dog?" one kid wanted to know. "To me, that's a dog. And that's a cat," I said, ignoring the rest of his remarks. On the Thursday before Easter, the last day of that school week, we had our party. "Put your heads down on your desks," said Miss García, adding, "I'm going outdoors to hide the eggs. When I whistle, everyone walk out in line. No running!"

But as soon as the whistle blew, we all ran out to the playground. We lined up outside and when she blew the whistle again, it was time to go hunt for the *cascarones* and place them in the bags she had given each of us. She had an extra bag of candy for the one who collected the most. We then went around breaking them on each other's head, as was the Mexican tradition. We made sure to run around breaking them on the heads of all the kids. Some children actually felt left out if no one broke eggs on their heads. Everyone always sought out the most popular kids. One kid reached up and broke one on Miss García's head. She didn't mind at all.

We also made a *piñata* with the help of Miss García. The girls wanted us to turn the *olla* into a doll. The boys wanted that old clay pot to be decorated as a boat. The teacher suggested a clown and showed us a picture of a clown that we all agreed looked good and would make a great *piñata*. On the day of our party, another boy and I climbed up a pole and hung the *piñata*. We all took turns being blindfolded and turned around several times before trying to reach it with a stick and break it. Meanwhile, Miss García kept moving it around with the rope we had tied to it to make it harder to break.

Finally one of the taller boys reached the *piñata* and broke it. All the candy came tumbling down and the whole class ran to grab as much as we could. We all thought the kid who broke it had cheated because his blindfold seemed to be too high on his forehead and he could see. But with all the candy on the ground, we didn't care.

As we scrambled for the spilled candy, it began to rain, which was very unusual in our area. We ran inside and continued with our party. In addition to our lunch, we enjoyed some cookies and lemonade two of the mothers had prepared for us. Miss García believed that as Mexican children, we should continue to practice some of our traditions, such as decorating Easter eggs and making and breaking *piñatas*. Besides, these were lots of fun and the children all enjoyed them. "This is not the end of Easter," she told us. "Make sure you go to church on Sunday. Make sure your parents take you."

On Easter Sunday, we arose before dawn. The baby goat we had welcomed in February was ready to become our Easter meal, since this was a very special day and we were getting some very special guests: my grandparents. Knowing how much I hated to see my little goat go, my father killed it before I woke. As I went outside to the outhouse, I could see him cutting it up and preparing it for our Easter meal.

"Don't be sad, Pedrito. It's a very special day. Your grandparents will soon be here, my son."

My father's parents, who had never been to our home, found a ride to San Pedro, a few miles upriver from where we lived, where they walked across the bridge that connects Texas to Mexico into Roma, where my father and I were waiting. Roma is about fifteen minutes upriver from Mr. Shaffer's farm, and we took his truck to pick them up. Before we could greet them, a crossing guard warned my grandparents, "Don't forget to come back early tonight." Their pass was good only for the day. They could not venture more than a few miles from the border, and the bridge closed at midnight, so they must return early enough to make the crossing.

The moment my grandparents crossed to where we waited, my grandmother ran to me and hugged me and kissed me what seemed like a dozen times. Her own son didn't get as many kisses.

We hurried home to pick up my mother and Elenita, and there were more tears and lots of talk and lots of hugs, particularly for

Elenita. We all went into the village for Easter Mass—with my mother and Elenita and me in the back of the truck so my grandparents could ride up front with my father. My grandmother was very short, and I wouldn't call her fat, but let's say she was stout and would never be able to jump in the back of the truck. My grandfather was very thin, so the three could sit, uncomfortably, in front, for the short ride to the church.

The Mass was very long and the church was very hot and crowded. Many of the men simply stood outside, glancing in through the doors and windows and trying to follow the Mass. Father Gustavo greeted us with open arms and reminded everyone during the sermon, "We're here every Sunday, my friends. We love seeing you for Easter and for Christmas, but don't forget us, don't forget God, the rest of the year."

On the way home, my grandmother started to hum *"Las Mañanitas."* She explained that in Mexico, it's a song for birthdays and holidays. My grandfather then started to sing and everyone joined in:

*Estas son las mañanitas, que cantaba el Rey David.*
*Hoy que es día de tu santo, te las cantamos a ti . . .*

"Oh, the songs of my youth, around the turn of the century," my grandmother said. "The many revolutions destroyed our country and our people, but produced some beautiful songs, *'Mi Amapola,' 'La Golondrina,' 'La Valentina.'"*

There was no holding my grandfather now as he started to sing:

*Valentina, Valentina, yo te quisiera decir . . .*

He forgot some of the words but picked up pieces here and there that didn't quite make sense:

*No le hace que seas de otro, yo tambien me se morir."*

He then remembered the songs that paid tribute to the great cities, like Guadalajara, not that he had ever visited them, and he sang snippets of them:

*Ay, Jalisco, no te rajes . . .*
*Guadalajara, Guadalajara . . .*

Since he hardly ever said much, much less sang, no one wanted to join in or help with the missing words, preferring just to listen. But we all applauded as we pulled into our ranch.

Once back home, my mother and grandmother, both still wearing their best dresses but with aprons over them, went to work, making tortillas and refried beans, cutting up vegetables, and talking about relatives and friends they had not seen in a long time.

"I wonder how Rubén and Marta are doing," said my grandmother, speaking of our cousins who were now probably in New Mexico, working in the fields.

"They are fine, or we would have heard," said my mother, as my grandmother nodded.

My father, grandfather, and I worked on the barbecue, although I couldn't shake off my feeling that in order for us to enjoy a good Easter dinner, my little goat had to be sacrificed.

Elenita distracted us all, singing and jumping and running back and forth from where we were barbecuing to where my mother and grandmother were cooking. I, too, went back and forth, listening to my father and his father talk, and then checking out my mother and grandmother's conversations.

During dinner, I wasn't really in the mood but, of course, my parents made me recite the "Pledge of Allegiance" and sing "My

Country 'Tis of Thee" to my grandparents. I let Elenita take care of the ABCs.

No one really noticed that I didn't touch the baby goat. I only had rice and beans and tamales and tortillas, but that was plenty.

"*Qué lindos hijos,*" said my grandmother. "*Qué lindos,*" added my grandfather. "I love the way they sing. And their English is so beautiful."

"You should teach them some Mexican songs also," said my grandmother to my mother.

"They are learning," said my mother. But my grandmother kept on talking. "I'm not an educated person, God knows, but '*Las Mañanitas*' is one of the most beautiful songs ever written. What other song tells you that the day you were born all the flowers in the world blossomed." Of course, she had to sing that part:

*El día que tu naciste*
*Nacieron todas las flores . . .*

But the day was fast coming to an end and it was time for my grandparents to return to Mexico. They had promised the man who drove them to the border they would be ready for him at six o'clock. This time my grandfather and I rode on the back of the truck to give my grandmother and father more room up front. But it was a short drive.

"One of these days," said my grandmother, "I want you and Elenita to come visit us and your other cousins and uncles and aunts in Mexico." I promised her I would, if my parents agreed.

There were more kisses, more tears, and more good-byes and many "*Hasta la vistas.*"

In many ways, I wished my grandparents lived across the street so I could get to know them better.

# Chapter 15

## What a Teacher, Miss García!

On the first day of school, two of the children in my class showed up barefoot. Miss García took them aside and told them they must wear shoes to school. I could tell from where I sat what she was talking about, although she spoke very quietly so the rest of us would not hear.

"*Qué pasa con* Miss García?" I asked Manuel, one of the barefoot kids.

"She said my sister Lucia and I must wear shoes, or we could hurt ourselves or catch some illness."

"Don't you have even one pair of shoes?"

"No, but next month, when the pumpkins are ready for the market, my father will have the money to buy some for me and my sister," said Manuel. Manuel was a year older than Lucia, but he hadn't gone to school the year before because his parents were on the road, picking fruit. That year, their parents decided to find a job locally, so the children could attend school.

Miss García sent a note to the parents, asking if the children could remain in school with her for an hour or so the following afternoon, saying she would drive them home. That afternoon, she took the children to the store and bought them shoes. She said nothing to anyone, but Manuel and Lucia came in wearing shoes the following day. Manuel smiled when he saw me and pointed down. "Miss García bought them for us," he said.

That's the way Miss García was. Always helping children. As the end of the school year drew closer, I feared losing her. "I don't think there will ever be another teacher like Miss García," I told my parents. She was always caring, protective, loving of all of us six-year-old Mexican kids. She tried very hard to teach us English, repeating words or phrases or songs or poems over and over. Some of the children never got it. Some of us learned faster than others. But she was always very patient. She seemed to understand we were the children of very humble, poor parents, most of whom had never gone to school and who hardly spoke any English.

Sometimes I wanted to burst out laughing when she tried desperately to get us to say something correctly: "No children, repeat after me. 'Thanks.' *Th. Th. Th.* Not *Ta.* Not *Ta Ta Ta* as in *tanks.* That's a different word, *niños.*" Once in a while Miss García forgot her rule and used a Spanish word in class, but she continued as if nothing had gone wrong. She always noticed, though, when one of us kids used a Spanish word. We were to speak only English, unless she directed, "Say it in Spanish," which she did when she knew it was the only way for us to get our point across.

After struggling with us, it was no wonder that a big smile covered her face when the bell rang and it was time for us to go outdoors and play. Miss García said she preferred playtime in the morning, particularly in the hotter months. By early April, the days were already hot and in May, the last month of school, one felt the heat in school all day. The windows were all open to the top, but it didn't seem to help. There was no air conditioning.

Our routine didn't vary much from one day to the other. After half an hour outdoors playing ball and running, the bell rang again. It was now noon, and we returned to our classroom. We lined up at the sink, washed our hands, took out our lunches, and ate. Miss García invariably looked at her watch. To no one in particular she exclaimed, "It's going to be a hot afternoon. Probably another hundred-degree day." Sometimes she folded the newspaper she always carried and fanned herself.

As we approached the last week of school, Miss García told me, "Pedrito, you're a good boy. I'm very pleased with your progress. Your parents should be very proud."

"I want to learn more numbers, Miss García. What comes after one thousand?" I asked her.

"Oh, Pedro, the count goes on forever. There are millions and then there are billions and trillions and more. There are numbers so big I can't imagine anything or anyone counting that high. I don't even know if I can count that high myself. Maybe only the person who counts all the pennies in all the banks knows. But you will learn the bigger numbers in the second and third grades. No need to hurry. You won't need them now." When I didn't seem to understand what she was saying, she would explain it all again in Spanish.

Miss García promised to lend me some books for the summer. "I will get you a couple of books," she said. "You can read one in early summer, and save the other for late summer. That way you will review some of the words you've learned, and it will help you when you start the second grade in September."

"What do you do in summer, Miss?" I wanted to know.

"I'm going away to college for six weeks," she said. "When I return, I will go to the ranch and visit you. If you have problems with the books, you can ask me then. If you've read the books, I will find you more."

I was surprised Miss García was still going to school and, thinking I heard wrong, I asked, "You go to school, Miss García?" I thought teachers knew everything.

"Of course, one can never and should never stop learning," she said, adding, "especially teachers."

I sometimes wondered if she was married and if she had any children. She was really too young to have children, I thought. She was too beautiful, thin and tall, with a lovely smile and her long brown hair. Most of the mothers I knew looked older and didn't wear such nice clothes that appeared store-bought.

Anyway, if she had children she would probably be home with them, not in school with us. Mothers didn't work, as far as I knew, except for cleaning, ironing, cooking, and taking care of their children, or helping their husbands on the farm.

"Maybe I'll ask my mother to ask Miss García if she is married when she comes around to visit this summer," I thought. I was never sure what my mother would say when I asked things like that. Knowing my mother, if she was in a good mood, she would say, "Of course, Pedrito, I will ask her." If not, she would simply say, "Pedro, it's none of your business." Miss García also promised to lend me her guitar for the summer. It was the guitar she played when we sang in class. I didn't know how to play, but my father said when he first came to Texas, he learned to play from his uncle. But his uncle's guitar was very old and the strings broke and were never fixed, so my father finally had to throw it away. I hoped he still remembered so he could teach me. We could then sing some of those Mexican songs he and my mother loved so much and would hum or sing all the time.

I can just hear them:

*Ay, Jalisco, no te rajes . . .*
*Mira como ando, mujer, por tu querer . . .*

*Estas son las mañanitas . . .*

And many more. Of course, we would also sing the songs I had learned in school all year long. I think my parents preferred their old Mexican songs, though, or so it seemed when my grandparents came to visit and everyone sang constantly.

As the summer approached, I often thought how much I would miss Miss García. I would miss her the following year, also. Too bad teachers didn't get promoted to the next grade with their students. On the other hand, that may not have been such a good idea. If you had a bad teacher, like some of my friends in the third grade, it could be a problem for the rest of your school days. For now, I just hoped for a teacher who would be as caring and would teach me as much as Miss García.

But she will always be my favorite teacher. Even if I liked my new teacher, I planned to always return to the first grade to visit Miss García.

# Chapter 16

## Welcome, Summer!

"Good morning, children," our principal Mrs. Davis said as she walked into our room on the last day of school.

"Good morning, Mrs. Davis," we all replied in unison, as we had been drilled to do when anyone entered the room.

She was there to hand us our report cards and to encourage us to continue with our studies. "You've graduated from the first grade, children. Next year you will be attending class across the hall," she added, pointing to her left. "Don't forget everything you've learned this year. See you next year, across the hall."

I thought about all the things I had learned, from the ABCs and the one, two, threes to "God Bless America." But this was the end of May and the weather was getting hotter and as much as I expected to miss school, I was ready to play and spend more time on the farm.

Miss García had prepared cookies and lemonade, and we all enjoyed them after Mrs. Davis left. As usual, Miss García accompanied us to the bus stop, where she hugged and kissed us all. Other students had already walked home or had been picked up by their parents or older brothers and sisters. As she said good-bye to me, she said, "I will come by your house Monday to bring you the books I promised." "And the guitar?" I wondered. "And the guitar," she said.

That day after school was not much different at home. My mother and my sister and I went to the river to do our wash, as usual. And as usual, we ran into Doña María.

"*¿Qué pasa?*" the old lady asked.

"*La niña,*" said my mother, explaining that Elenita had complained about an earache the night before.

"Don't worry," said Doña María, "if she complains again, warm up a little chicken fat and put it in her ear. She'll never complain again."

"Right," I thought, "I wouldn't either."

Our old *burro* never complained about anything, and off he went up the road with our clean laundry. He was getting old, and unless we found another one, I would probably be the one hauling the laundry back and forth to the river as I got older and stronger. I loved that old *burro,* as I loved our goats, Topo and Tita. You couldn't really love the chickens or the pigs. They didn't even know you existed.

As promised, on the Monday after school ended, Miss García showed up at our farm and talked to my mother about the need for me to practice some of my first grade exercises.

"Pedrito, I know how you love animals, so I picked up a copy of *Black Beauty,* about a beautiful horse, so you can read during the summer. It's a little hard for your age, but I think you can handle it. Underline the words you don't understand and we'll discuss them when I return from summer school." I was afraid the book was too advanced for me, but I told her I would try to read it. Maybe someone could help me with the difficult words, although I couldn't ask my parents or Doña María. Oh well. I'd figure something out.

"Oh," said Miss García, "if you finish that one, here's another one. *Heidi* is about a little girl who lives in a country where there is lots of snow. I remember how thrilled you were to learn about snow. I think you'll like it."

She told me those two books would be enough for now. "That'll give you time to play the guitar," she said as she handed me the beautiful, shiny instrument that I had been eyeing since her arrival.

The summer evenings grew longer and we spent more time outdoors. On one of those evenings, my mother said to me: "I need to cut your hair very short." After finishing with me, she turned to my father: "Your turn." Neither of us objected. My father and I usually kept our hair very short, anyway. My mother's hair was long, almost to her shoulders, very black, very straight, and very shiny. But she usually wore it in a bun at the back of her head. I liked it when she let her hair loose, but she said she preferred it in a bun, "otherwise it gets all over my face, especially when I'm cooking."

In the summertime, the weather was usually comfortable from the time the sun set until it came out again in the morning. The evenings were longer in the summer and we could do much of our work after the sun had set but before the moon had shown its face. Forget about the middle of the day, when it was always very hot. There was no getting work done then!

"We must water the plants early in the morning," my father reminded me. "Midday water boils them and cooks them. And we don't want to cook them while they're still in the field." My mother and I did most of the work tending our vegetables, for my father was busy working for Mr. Shaffer all day.

Every day we tended to our tomatoes and *calabacitas* and corn and green beans. And all summer long I kept an eye on our watermelon patch. I could hardly wait for those watermelons to grow nice and juicy. I kept dreaming of the day early in September when my father and I would return to San Antonio with our fresh crop of watermelons, around the time I would be returning to school and entering the second grade.

I enjoyed working on the garden, but I also found time to practice my letters and numbers, and I started to read the books Miss García left for me.

I always felt very sorry for people who could not or would not read. I vowed that when I grew up, I would have many books in my home. I would lend them to all the children who wanted to read. My mother and father grew up without books. I can't blame their parents. Survival was their only aim. Food was important. Books cost money, and every penny had to be saved for buying food.

In our home we actually had one book, other than mine, but it was very difficult to read, and it was in Spanish, so it was impossible for me. It was the Bible and it was given to my mother by a man and woman who came to our house one day to invite us to join their church. My mother told them we were Catholic, but she invited them to sit in our front yard. She served them coffee and bean tacos.

"They were a very lovely couple, very religious, even if they weren't Catholic," said my mother. When they left, they offered my mother and our family their blessings, and my mother said, "May our dear Lady of Guadalupe protect you on your journey." They thanked her but the lady said to my mother, "No, no, we don't pray to Our Lady of Guadalupe. We only ask God for protection." My mother thought that was strange. They offered my mother a copy of the Bible and my mother accepted it.

"It's a good book, the word of God," my mother said the lady told her, adding, "Every home should have one." My father, who read Spanish, with difficulty, sometimes looked at the Bible and even quoted from it when he found what he considered "beautiful words." Some of it was very difficult to understand, he said. "It's Spanish, but it's very formal or very old Spanish, I don't know which," he explained. He was a very slow reader and sometimes struggled to pronounce the words.

But he did notice one particular word. "Your name is in the Bible, Pedro," said my father, who explained that "Pedro was the most important apostle to Jesus."

"What's an apostle?"

"Oh, it's sort of a helper; he was something like the *mayordomo* to Jesus. When Jesus died, he left Pedro in charge, a very important job."

"Is that why you and *Mamacita* called me Pedro, *Papá?*"

"Not really, but maybe partly," said my mother. "You see, your father had an uncle who was a very strong and very intelligent man. He could read everything, and he wrote beautiful poetry. They even wanted him to be a teacher at one time. His name was Pedro and I think the priest suggested the same, as in San Pedro."

"Could he read and write English?"

"Well, no," said my father, "only Spanish. But he lived in Mexico. He would have been a great man, but unfortunately he died very young. He was not even thirty years old when he died. We don't know what was wrong. He just got sick one day, couldn't eat. He lost a lot of weight. Suddenly one morning, they found him dead."

"When I grow older I hope to read the Bible and other great books," I told my parents. "Do I have to learn to read Spanish to read the Bible?"

"No," said my mother, "you can read the Bible and other great books in many languages. But you should one day learn to read Spanish, too."

For the coming summer, I'd stick to the books Miss García loaned me. The words I didn't know I saved for Miss García, who would explain them to me later.

It was a very hot summer, but I was having a good time.

# Afterword

The events in *Pedrito's World* are true, as far as my memory of events that happened more than sixty years ago can recall. But I would be doing my readers a disservice to vow that every event and situation is exactly as it happened. This is why, instead of making this a collection of essays and anecdotes, I invented Pedrito and his family.

I was encouraged by my wife, Pat, to put the events of those childhood days down on paper. But I needed an angle and an anchor. By creating the character Pedrito, I could tell some of those stories more coherently through his eyes. Pedrito is a composite of three or four kids I knew, including myself. His parents and other characters in the book are also composites.

For narrative purposes, I needed to pare down my family to two children (we were eight). The main character had to be the older of the two and had to be a boy. He had to be from the farm because trying to separate country and a rural city in the minds of the urban readers would be a difficult task. And he had to be more innocent than I felt, in retrospect, that I was at the age of six. I was born and reared in town, rural as it was; Pedrito came from the country. My family had settled in Texas years ago, while I wanted to explore the life of a child whose family had arrived recently from Mexico. My parents were merchants; Pedrito's were farm workers. I knew some

*My father Gabriel—
probably age 21, around
1916.*

*Funeral for one of my grandparents, probably around 1930. The school in*
Pedrito's World *is in the background close to the church.*

English when I entered the first grade, Pedrito didn't know a word. Thus I needed Pedrito to relate the struggles of learning English for the children around me.

Once I had Pedrito, I needed a time frame. Many of the events that were so vividly embedded in my memory took place in 1941. I wanted to relate the stories about having to put out the lights at night for fear that the Germans were flying over us. There were those wonderful evenings when I sat in our market with my father and my uncle and other adults, and we listened to the Joe Louis boxing championships on the radio. That was the summer I spent with my aunt and uncle in a farm upriver, which became the prototype for Pedrito's farm. That was the year I went with my aunt and uncle to the river to bathe and to wash our clothes and to communicate with people across the river.

Many of these stories popped into my mind when my own children were growing up. Curious as children are, they would frequently ask me to tell them stories about my childhood days in a world far removed from their own. I was born and reared in a poor, rural, Mexican-American community in south Texas. They came from an urban, middle-class environment outside New York City.

They wanted to know about their ancestors, so I told them about my great-grandmother who was bitten by a deadly snake but survived. I told them about the great-grandfather who went to Laredo by horseback to pickup supplies but didn't return for more than a month and everyone thought he was dead. They loved those stories of survival in the hot Texas frontier.

They also laughed when I talked about the adventures of outhouses. They marveled at *cascarones,* the Easter eggs, and made me make some for them. They loved the stories about the pigs and little lambs and goats that grew up in our backyard, and those Victory vegetable gardens we grew. I told them about growing up in a meat

*My father, in front of his store, probably in 1941. The room at right, the original part of the house, is where all his children were born. It eventually became part of the store.*

*Martina Martinez and her sons (from right) Lisandro, Joel, Arturo, Rubén, and Gabriel with his wife, Francisca, probably 1956.*

market, helping to butcher animals by the time I was six, working in the store all my childhood days. They were saddened when I spoke about an older brother who died of pneumonia after catching a cold while tending to his little lambs, another story that found its way into *Pedrito's World*.

When I retired after spending all my adult life as a journalist dealing with facts, I decided I wanted to try the challenges of writing a novel. But those facts, those memories of my childhood days would not disappear from my mind. I wanted to use that material with the tools of a novelist. Hence, this fictive memoir.

So a year in the life of Pedrito worked well in my narrative. Events from other years will have to wait for another story, as I continue to explore my memory of those childhood days. Too many of us from that era are no longer around to tell their tales. Those of us who have some memories left must avail ourselves of opportunities to leave those memories to future generations.

AM

# Glossary

**agua para el niño**   water for the child

**Ahora**   now is the time

**Algo pasa**   Something's happening

**arroyo**   gully, water hole, stream

**Ave María, Madre de Dios, ruega por nosotros los pecadores . . .**   Hail Mary, Mother of God, pray for us sinners . . .

**Ay, Dios mio, donde está . . .**   My dear God, where is . . .

**Ay, hijos, le hicieron ojo**   Oh, children, they cast an evil eye (on her)

**Ay, qué huele bueno** Oh, how good it smells

**¿Ay, qué es eso?**   Oh, what is that?

**Ay, qué guapo, qué bueno**   Oh, how helpful (handy), how good

**Ay, qué linda[o] está**   Oh, how wonderful (good) it is

**bandidos**   bandits, criminals

**burrito**   term of endearment, or "little donkey"

**burro**   donkey

**calabacitas**   zucchini, pumpkins, "little squash"

**cascarones**   egg shells decorated for Easter

**chicharrones**   fried pig skins, "cracklings"

**compadre**   a real friend

**contratista**   contractor, freelancer

**corazón**   heart, sweetheart

**curandera**   female faith (folk) healer

**¿De dónde vienen?**   Where are you coming from?

**Diosito**   Dear God

**Dios mío, Dios mío, qué mal tiempo**   Dear God, Dear God, what bad times

**el niño**   the boy

**El Padre Nuestro que estás en el Cielo . . .**   Our Father who art in Heaven . . .

**Eres tú?**   Is it you?

**este niño**   this child

**federales**   federal soldiers

**hasta el año que viene**   until next year

**hasta la vista**   goodbye; until I see you

**hijito**   term of endearment for *hijo,* or "little son"

**hijo**   son

**hombre**   man

**hora**   hour

**jefe**   boss

**jefecita**   boss, or a term of endearment as "little boss"

**La Noche Buena**   Christmas Eve, literally "the good night"

**mamacita**   term of endearment for *mamá*

**marqueta**   market (grocery store)

**masa**   dough

**mayordomo**   majordomo, butler, steward

**menudo**   stew

**mira, mi amor**   look, my love

**mucha nieve, mucho frío**   lots of snow, lots of cold (weather)

**mujer**   woman

**muy bien**   very well

**no, sólo mas**   no, nothing else

**olla**   the jar for the piñata

**olor**   smell, odor

**padrecito**   term of endearment for father; in this case, the priest

**papito**   term of endearment for *papá*, also *papacito*

**piñata**   decorated pottery jar filled with candy

**pobrecitos**   poor (little boys)

**¿Porqué, querida?**   Why, dear?

**primitos**   term of endearment for *primos*

**primos**   first cousins

**pues sí, amigo**   of course, friend

**Que Dios les (or te) bendiga**   May God bless you

**qué dulce**   how sweet

**¿Qué es?**   What is it?

**¿Qué es 'Miss' y todo eso?**   What is "Miss" and all that?

**que lindos hijos**   what wonderful children

**¿Qué llevas?**   What are you carrying?

**¿Qué pasa?**   What's happening?

**querida**   loved one

**Qué vayan con . . .**   May you go with . . .

**ranchos**   ranches, farms

**sandías**   watermelons

**siéntate**   sit down

**taquitos**   little tacos

**tía**   aunt

**tío**   uncle

**Vamos a jugar**   Let's go play

**¿Verdad?**   Isn't it true? or, Is that right?

**Ya no llores**   Don't cry anymore; Stop crying

## Songs

*Chapter 1*

**Allá en el rancho grande, allá donde vivía**
**Había una rancherita, que alegre me decía . . .**
**¿Qué te decía, hombre?**

Over at the big ranch, over where I lived
There was a cowgirl, who joyfully used to tell me . . .
What did she tell you?

*Chapter 14*

**Estas son las mañanitas que cantaba el Rey David,**
**Hoy que es día de tu santo, te las cantamos a ti.**
**El día que tu naciste, nacieron todas las flores.**

These are the greetings that King David used to sing,
Now on this your birthday, we dedicate them to you.
The day you were born, all the flowers bloomed.

**Valentina, Valentina, yo te quisiera decir . . .**
**No le hace que seas de otro, yo también me se morir.**

Valentina, Valentina, here's what I want you to know . . .
No matter that you belong to another, (I can assure you) I know
how to die (for your love).

**Ay, Jalisco, no te rajes.**

Oh, Jalisco, don't give up.

*Chapter 15*

**Mira como ando, mujer, por tu querer . . .**

Look at my (drunken) state, woman, due to my love for you . . .